"You can ... here."

Oh, yeah? Watch me. I long to say the words, but my throat feels like it's closing up.

"How can you do this, Summer?" Skye glares at me, her chin jutting forward. "I *cannot* believe you're leaving...." She puts her hands on her temples, like the drama queen she is. "No, wait, yes, I can. It's just like you to hightail it when things are tough."

Oh. I'm tempted to slug her. My mouth is so dry, but I manage to choke out, "Now you wait just a minute."

Skye throws up her hands. "Go your merry way and leave it all to me. You are undoubtedly the most selfish woman I've ever known."

All I can think of as I watch her walk away is *No one knows you like a sister.*

Unless your sister doesn't know you at all.

Nancy Robards Thompson

Award-winning author Nancy Robards Thompson is a sister, wife and mother who has lived the majority of her life south of the Mason-Dixon line. As the oldest sibling, she reveled in her ability to make her brother laugh at inappropriate moments and soon learned she could get away with it by proclaiming, "What? I wasn't doing anything." It's no wonder that upon graduating from college with a degree in journalism, she discovered that reporting "just the facts" bored her silly. Since hanging up her press pass to write novels full-time, critics have deemed her books "...funny, smart and observant." She loves chocolate, champagne, cats and art (though not necessarily in that order). When she's not writing, she enjoys spending time with her family, reading, hiking and doing yoga.

Nancy Robards Thompson

SISTERS

copyright © 2006 by Nancy Robards Thompson

i s b n   0 3 7 3 8 8 0 9 6 0

This edition published by arrangement with Harlequin Books S.A.

® and TM are trademarks of the publisher. Trademarks indicated with
® are registered in the United States Patent and Trademark Office, the
Canadian Trade Marks Office and in other countries.

TheNextNovel.com

HARLEQUIN®

PRINTED IN U.S.A.

From the Author

Dear Reader,

Before I started writing fiction full-time, I worked as a reporter for a Central Florida business newspaper. While there, I wrote a story about a local chef who'd organized a food bank that served the area's homeless shelters and soup kitchens. Talking to him was a real eye-opener. He pointed out that in many cases people don't choose homelessness because they're lazy, that often mental illness plays a large role in the downward spiral that lands someone on the streets.

In my book *Sisters*, which is adapted from my manuscript that won the 2002 Romance Writers of America Golden Heart Award, a mother and her twin daughters set out on a road trip to find the youngest sister, who ran away from home when she was sixteen and chose to live on the streets despite numerous offers of family help. In the process, they confess secrets that heal wounds that have kept them apart for years and discover how compassion and understanding can lead to a richer purpose in life.

I hope you are inspired by their journey and that life brings you many blessings.

Warmly,

Nancy Robards Thompson

This book is dedicated to my wonderful brother,
Jay Robards, whose gentle ways and compassionate heart
set an example we should all live by. Thanks for helping me
with the details of homelessness and shelters.
Jay, your work changes lives. I am so proud of you.

Thanks to Gail Chasan and Tara Gavin for seeing
the vision in my work; and to Michelle Grajkowski for your
sage advice and unwavering support.
Thanks to my father, Jim Robards, for mapping
out the route from Florida to Missouri.
Thanks to Robin Trimble and Susan Pettegrew for
educating me on the ups and downs of bipolar disorder.
Thanks to Pamela LaBud for teaching me
about coma recovery.
Deepest appreciation to Brock and Sarah McClane
for input on fractures.
Love and thanks to Teresa Brown, Kathy Garbera,
Elizabeth Grainger, Catherine Kean and
Mary Louise Wells for reading chapters at a moment's notice,
for helping me when I've plotted myself into a corner
and for your constant friendship.
As always, deepest love to Michael and Jennifer.
You make my life complete.

CHAPTER 1

Skye

Most people aren't doing anything special when bad news barges in. It's usually just a regular day.

The call comes on an ordinary Monday. The kids are at school. My husband, Cameron, is at work. I'm bringing in groceries from the SUV, hurrying because it's going to rain. I can smell the showers moving in, that loamy-earth scent of decay and renewal, wafting from the back burner of summer's last days.

I set the plastic bags on the granite-topped island in the kitchen and turn to go back out for the rest when the phone rings. I almost don't pick up. But something—I'd call it a sixth sense, if I believed in such hooey—compels me to answer.

"Hello?"

"May I talk to Skye Woods?"

It's a man's voice I don't recognize. Traces of a Spanish accent. I'm guessing he's a solicitor and I get ready to tell him that we're on the State of Florida's *Do Not Call* list, that his company could receive a hefty fine.

"Who is calling, please?"

"Skye, it is Raul Martinez."

My breath catches. Raul is Mama's personal assistant. He's a jack-of-all-trades, keeping her appointments for the foundation she's set up to help the needy and making sure her life runs in order.

His voice is tight and low, and it raises gooseflesh on my arms. The spaces between his words hint at something ominous, like the angry clouds rolling in across the flat afternoon sky. I walk over to the sink and stare out the window.

It's getting darker outside. The interior light of my vehicle glows like a beacon reminding me I left the lift gate open.

"There was an accident. Your mama, she is not doing so well."

My hand flutters to my cheek and a strange tingling erupts inside me as if his words cut the vein of decades of bad blood built up between Mama and me. In an instant the poison rushes out of me like watershed, and I hear myself stammering. "Oh my—is she okay? Raul, is she alive?"

As I grip the edge of the sink, beads of rain on the window come into sharp focus. It makes patterns that shape-shift each time a drop breaks free. I get the strangest sensation that each time it changes, another minute of Mama's life has slipped away...if she's not already dead.

"It's too early to tell," Raul says. "She is in a coma. So you should get here pretty fast."

I can't believe this. *Mama.* In a coma? Ginny, hippie mother earth—the eternal free spirit who collected love children like genetic souvenirs. But in all fairness, Summer and I are twins. So technically, Mama only got pregnant twice. Still, no matter how you slice it, there's nothing normal about having two different men father your children when you have no idea of one man's identity. Last time I asked, she had it narrowed down to a list of about ten or fifteen candidates.

"After all, the sixties was the era of free love," she always said. "At least I gave you life."

But that's not the issue right now. All of that and

the upheaval it's caused seem so insignificant in the face of…this.

I realize Raul just said something and is waiting for me to answer.

"I beg your pardon?"

"Can you telephone your sisters? I cannot find their numbers. The doctor said the next twenty-four hours are critical. So if you are coming, you should get here as fast as possible."

Summer

I haven't been back to Dahlia Springs in twenty-two years. Frankly, I haven't had the time, money or the inclination. But when my sister, Skye, calls to inform me that our mother's in a coma… Oh God.

What choice do I have? And it couldn't come at a worse time.

I suppose if I were completely honest, I'd admit I *don't want* to go home. Because Dahlia Springs isn't home. Never was.

My home is here in New York. My job is here, my friends are here.

Who was it that said friends are the family you choose?

Whoever it was hit it dead on. I wouldn't choose my family if I had the choice. But for some masochistic reason, I can't cast them off, either. Despite the fact that my sister and I don't see eye-to-eye on most issues. And our mother, Ginny, has had long-standing differences with Skye and me over the years.

Still, she's my mother. That's why I decide to purchase a plane ticket I can't afford and travel to a place I don't care to visit. Because the woman with whom relations have been strained at the best times and worse on other occasions is lying in a hospital bed in a coma.

"It might be a couple of days before I can get there. I may have to work a couple of days to give Gerard time to make arrangements. He's behind schedule with the spring collection and—"

"Summer, I don't think you understand the gravity of the situation." Skye's pitch veers into a sharp upper register and she's slipped into that drawl she uses when she's irritated, which is more often than not when we talk. "Mama may not last *a couple of days.*"

My stomach clenches, and I take a deep breath.

"Look, I'll get there as fast as I can. I'd be there now if I could. But I can't just drop everything. I have a job. I need to make arrangements for Gerard to get someone in here to fill in for me."

I don't have a husband to support me.

"What about Jane?" Skye asks. "Don't you think we owe it to her to tell her about Mama?"

The irony of Skye's words makes me laugh, but it sounds brittle. Even to my own ears. "Isn't that the story of her life? The whole damn world *owes* Jane, the one who's had everything."

Jane is our younger sister. Half sister, to be exact. We share the same mother. Ginny married Chester Hamby, Jane's father, after she got pregnant. Skye and I were nineteen and out of the house. So really it was a different chapter in Ginny's life. A chapter from which we were largely absent.

Our little sister's had all the advantages we didn't have growing up—a father for one. And a wealthy father to boot.

Before Chester met Ginny, he made millions off an invention—something to do with farming. I was never clear on what the gadget was, but it brought in a boatload of money.

Jane's twenty-one and to say she's a handful is an understatement. She ran away from home the first time when she was fourteen, about six months after her father died. She stayed away about a month. Of course, Ginny welcomed her home like the prodigal daughter. I can understand that. Jane was upset over losing her dad. Ginny was glad to have one of her daughters back.

But then Jane did it again when she was sixteen. Said she was going downtown. Three days later she called Ginny from New Orleans to tell her she'd gone on the road with her boyfriend, Rad Farley, and his band, Flaming Skeleton, to be the "wardrobe mistress."

Ha. It didn't take a genius to conclude that "wardrobe mistress" was really just code for glorified rock-and-roll groupie.

Ginny was beside herself and called begging me to do something. When I wouldn't go rushing down to New Orleans to whisk Jane back to Florida, my mother took all her anger out on *me*. I was in New York, for God's sake. And to be honest, if Ginny was even half the mother to Jane that she was to Skye and me, I didn't blame Jane for wanting to get the hell away from her.

Even though I want to be irritated with Skye for pressuring me to drop everything and come, a pang of guilt needles me. The truth is, it won't be that difficult for my boss to replace me while I'm away.

For the past seventeen years, I've been a house model for the designer Gerard Geandeau. The oh-so-glamorous job boils down to serving as a human mannequin on whom he fits his samples. It requires spending hours a day, nearly naked on my aching feet. Not a plum modeling job by any standard. Still, there's plenty of fresh meat clamoring for my position.

Gerard was not very compassionate about my asking for time off. He had no time to listen to my reasons.

Accident-smaccident. He had no sympathy.

It's the studio's busiest time of year, planning the spring collections. Work cannot come to a screeching halt because I must take personal leave for something so trivial as my mother being in a coma.

He didn't say it that way, but he might as well have. He's always been the temperamental creative type, prone to temper tantrums and flippant remarks, but he's never thrown a flaming arrow at me.

His lack of understanding hurt.

As a compromise, I stay so he can finish the piece he's fitted to me. It's two days later before I get to Dahlia Springs.

I hope once I get back, he won't have decided to keep my replacement on permanently, leaving me out in the cold.

Sometimes when the spotlight hits just right, all the style and beauty can't disguise that the under-belly of the fashion world is a very ugly place.

I'm reminded daily that I am a forty-year-old woman competing with fresh-faced babies. Just the other day, I was talking to an eighteen-year-old who came into the studio for a fashion-shoot fitting. She couldn't believe I was still modeling at *my age*.

"How have you managed to work so long?" It was all she could do to keep her mouth from gaping. "I'm not half as old as you and my agency's telling me to lie about my age."

She hasn't even hit her stride as a woman and already she's over the hill. Where does that put me?

"That's why you're doing the print work and they fit samples on me in the back room," I told her. "Just don't get fat and you'll get work."

And don't get old.

I didn't say that. But it's the truth. I was young and hot once. To be working at forty, I'm the exception, not the rule. I have no idea how I've managed to pull it off this long. Every day I wake up fearing the other Manolo will drop.

Sometimes I detest this business. But what else would I do with myself?

Skye picks me up from Dahlia Springs Municipal Airport. It's the first time we've seen each other since she and her husband, Cameron, and their gaggle of kids came up to visit. How long has it been now— five years?

Waiting to disembark the small commuter plane, I stand last in line behind the ten people who were on my connecting flight from Atlanta. Who would've thought such a crowd had reason to come to Dahlia Springs? Had the entire population been on a field trip?

Everyone except for Nick Russo, my ex-husband.

My stomach pitches at the thought of being within miles of him. Okay, I'll confess, I've never gotten over him. I'm not morose about it, but of all the guys I've been with since Nick and I split up eight years ago, none has compared.

It's like being infected with a virus (as unromantic as that sounds). For the most part, I live a satisfying life—have the occasional date or lover, and then comes the Nick outbreak and I realize I'm better off on my own.

I called him to let him know I was coming.

To warn him? Ha.

But he did sound happy to hear from me, even suggested we get together.

Oh, God, it's been a long time.

Don't get too carried away. People change.

Yes, they certainly do.

I'm dying for a cigarette, but I know it might be a while, since you can't light up inside the airport, and I know Skye will have a fit if I ask her to wait while I smoke.

I take a deep breath and hitch my purse up on my shoulder, mentally preparing myself for what I'm about to walk into. Like a prisoner marching to her death, I follow the person in front of me as we walk single file down the metal steps onto the tarmac.

Humidity envelops me, and I can feel my hair expanding with each stride across the hot pavement. It's hot in New York, but God, there's nothing like the Deep South in the dead heat of August.

Geographically speaking, Dahlia Springs is in north Florida—just over the Georgia line, but it's the unofficial southernmost border of the *Deep South*. That's not an insult. The fine people of Dahlia Springs pride themselves on being the deepest of the Deep South.

As you travel farther into Florida, the less *Southern* it becomes, until around Fort Lauderdale, it's almost as if you've crossed the border into a different country.

When I finally enter the tiny airport, it's eerie how it looks exactly as it did that day I flew out all those years ago. It even smells the same—a blend of Juicy Fruit gum, jet fuel and floor wax—for a moment, it takes me back to the day I left. That day when for the first time in my life, the world held so much possibility.

Well, Toto, I'm certainly not in Oz anymore. It's confirmed when I look over and see Skye waiting for me on the other side of a cordoned-off area that separates the gates—all two of them—from ticketing and baggage claim.

There she is: Skye Woods, my twin sister. Once

upon a time we looked so much alike people couldn't tell us apart, but that's where the similarity ends. We're as different inside as summer and winter. In fact, I always used to tease that Ginny misnamed Skye. She should have called her Winter. Apply that any way you choose....

Yes, we're that different. We never had that twin-bonding thing going on; never could read each other's minds; never shared a secret twin language or anything cute like that. Until we were about six years old, Ginny used to dress us alike—as if we were her very own living baby dolls. But right around that time is when everything changed, including my sister and me.

Skye sees me walking toward her, but she doesn't smile. Oh, great. For a split second I worry that she has bad news, but there's something in her icy expression that says she's mad because I didn't drop everything and get here sooner.

I did the best I could. She better get over it.

She's changed her hair. It's a brick-red bob. The color reminds me of the redhead on *Desperate Housewives*. That character always makes me think of my perfect sister and her Southern belle Cinderella existence.

Skye's life seems like a ball and chain to me. I'd take being happily single—well, unhappily *divorced*—and living in the city over her perfect life, with her perfect lawyer husband in their perfect three-quarters-of-a-million-dollar Tallahassee ivory tower. Her existence is so—perfect—even Martha Stewart would gag.

Unfair of me, I know. I guess that makes me the evil twin. That's fine.

"I'm glad you could *finally* make it." She leans in and air-kisses my left cheek. "Let's get your bags and we'll go right to the hospital."

"How's Ginny? Any change?"

She shakes her head. "Mama's still the same. We'll talk to the doctor when we get there. He's usually in around three o'clock."

A sound like a foghorn blasts, signaling that the baggage is ready to start its turn around the carousel. Skye walks ahead of me toward it.

As I follow, I notice with perverse satisfaction my sister's put on weight since the last time I saw her. She's a little fuller in the hips. Her waist is less defined. I suppose that's what happens after popping out three kids.

It's a wonder she hasn't had *work* done. You

know—a nip here, a tuck there. She and Cameron have the money.

Since they can afford it, my sister's probably staunchly against it. I'm just surprised Cameron hasn't insisted. A high-profile attorney doesn't want a fat wife.

Skye turns around and catches me eyeing her.

"What's wrong?"

I shake my head. "You look…tired. Are you okay?"

She smoothes a strand of hair behind her ear, smiles her gracious Junior League smile. "I'm fine. Just concerned about Mama."

My bag appears around the bend and I grab it.

As we walk out the door into the muggy Dahlia Springs afternoon, a feeling of dread washes over me. Coming home is going to be harder than I ever imagined. Maybe that's because no matter how I've tried to kid myself since I purchased the ticket, I know you can't go home again.

Skye

On the trip from the airport to the hospital, the conversation goes something like this:

Summer (digging in her purse): "Do you mind if I smoke?"

Me (gripping the steering wheel at ten and two): "You can't smoke in here."

Out of my peripheral vision I see her pull out one of those nasty things despite my request. She doesn't say anything for a few beats, just looks at me like she smells poop on my shoe.

My blood pressure rises. If she has the audacity to light up in my SUV, I will stop this vehicle and put her out along the side of the road.

Summer (sighing a long, exasperated sigh): "Fine."

Me (offering nothing but a short, oh-well shrug): "If it's so darned urgent, why didn't you have a smoke before we got in the car?"

She doesn't put the cigarette away. She fidgets with it as she stares out the passenger window. Her silence annoys me, and I know I shouldn't say it, but—"I can't believe you're still smoking. I'm sure I don't have to tell you how bad it is for you."

"No, you don't." Her words are a warning.

I smooth a wrinkle out of my polished cotton skirt. I know the cigarette lecture presses her buttons. But she's pressing *mine* sitting there so smug in her haute couture with her expensive haircut—I'm sure it's expensive. I can just tell. The color's beautiful—shiny, rich mink with chestnut highlights. And it's a good cut, even if the style's too long for a forty-year-old woman.

I know what I pay to have my hair done in Tallahassee—certainly not New York City prices—and that costs a pretty penny. I don't begrudge my sister her luxuries, but I do take issue with her taking her sweet time when I asked her to come to the table during a family emergency. Still, she's here. That's all that matters.

I turn on the radio. Willie Nelson's "Georgia On My Mind" is playing.

"Did you know Nick's back in town?" she says.

I dart a glance at her. She's looking at me with eyes just like mine—same shape, same slightly faded shade of green-blue.

A shiver courses through me.

"I didn't know that."

I do know he's here. Mama told me, but I don't care. I relax my grip on the steering wheel and signal before I turn left onto Orange Peel Street.

"I just thought you might like to know."

Well, you thought wrong. I don't give a darned dried apple about your ex-husband's whereabouts.

Why would she bring up Nick? Because I won't let her smoke? Well, too bad.

She twirls the cigarette between her fingers. The odor of tobacco and her spicy perfume waft toward me. There's another note in the air I can't quite put my finger on, but if I had to name it I'd call it *eau de holier-than-thou.*

I stop at a red light and steady myself before I look at her. "Are you going to look him up?" Even as much as I don't want to know, I want to know.

"Maybe for a conjugal visit."

Well, that's vulgar. "Maybe not. I heard he's involved with someone." I don't know if he is or not. I just say it to be spiteful and I know I should be ashamed of myself. I don't know why this unbearable urge to one-up my sister takes over when we're together.

Summer snorts. It's amazing what she can imply in the resonance of a single, unladylike sound. Suggestions that tempt me to retort, *Why, are you still trying to rub my nose in the fact that you stole him from me? That was another lifetime ago and you're not even together anymore.*

And Cameron and I are happily married.

The light turns green. I accelerate too fast, and the SUV bucks a little bit as I let off the gas pedal.

We ride in silence past the red Ford pickup that was broken down at the side of the road when I got into town two days ago. It's still stalled in the same place. For all I know it's been there years; past the Dairy Queen where I count five cars in the parking lot—the same Dairy Queen Mama used to take us to if she was in a good mood when we were kids; past the old Bargain Bin Dollar Store with the neon *S* that's burned out so it reads Dollar *tore*. Was it always like that? I can't remember.

Dahlia Springs looks every bit the same as it did when we were kids—like it's stuck in a time warp. Oh, but a lot's changed. Things that go way deeper than burned-out signs and Nick Russo and growing up and pretending you've moved on.

I take a deep breath, determined to change the subject. "I found Jane." I glance at my sister to gauge her reaction. She stares back at me with wide eyes, surprise washing her face clean of contempt.

"How'd you find her? Where is she?"

"She's in Springvale, Missouri. She's living in a homeless shelter."

CHAPTER 2

Skye

Summer goes pale. "Oh, God. I don't know why I'm surprised. Do we need to send her money so she can get here?"

I take a deep breath. "I didn't talk to her."

My sister looks at me as if I have two heads. "Why not? She needs to know about Ginny."

"I thought that if she knew we'd found her she might bolt. I wanted to talk to you so we could figure out a plan."

By the time we get to the hospital, we've reached no conclusions. We can't go get her ourselves on account of something possibly happening to Mama while we're gone. We want to be here. We can't send Raul or Cameron after her (not that Cameron has time to go traipsing after my wayward little sister), because there's no way she'd come back with them. In fact, she'd probably run.

A letter or a telegram?

Perhaps. But we'll talk about that later.

We walk to the elevator, which lifts us up to the third-floor ICU. I wave hello to the head nurse, a heavyset, fiftyish woman with graying hair and horn-rimmed glasses.

As we approach, the door to Mama's room opens and Dr. Travis leads his gaggle of med students out. He greets us, instructs his charges on what to do while he talks to us, then pauses, looking askance at Summer.

Summer flips her long, dark hair off her shoulder in that sultry way of hers. She's always had the ability to render men stupid—including Nick, though it didn't take much when it came to him.

I don't know whether it's some sort of pheromone she emits or if it's a gene that she got a double helping of and I got none.

"Dr. Travis, this is my sister, Summer Russo. She's just flown into town."

As she slips her French-manicured fingers into his outstretched hand, I notice a certain flash in the good doctor's eyes—like a power surge that makes the electricity burn brighter for a brief moment before it falls back into normal range.

Mama's nice-looking, young, *married* doctor is not impervious to my sister's wiles and that irritates the soup out of me.

"Where are you from?" he asks.

Her silver bangles clatter as she pulls her hand from his and crosses her arms under her ample chest. Boobs too big for her skinny little body. She was flat as a board the last time I saw her. Where did she get those?

"Manhattan."

He smiles and nods.

The good doctor hasn't as much as spared me a second glance. Not that it matters. I mean, I *am* happily married. And he's married—happily or otherwise. It's just that before Summer arrived, I didn't notice that he hadn't looked at me. You know, in that appreciative way a man looks at a woman he finds…attractive.

I stand up straighter, shoulders back and suck in my stomach.

As they make small talk, his gaze darts to the bounty thrusting out of her red silk blouse. I'll bet her cleavage is compliments of one of those water bras I've heard so much about. If she had implants installed, wouldn't it throw off her mannequinlike proportions? And wouldn't it interfere with her job? And wouldn't it be too bad if she had an accidental collision with a hypodermic needle and sprang a leak?

I have to bite the insides of my cheeks to keep from smiling at the thought. Oh, shame on me.

Positive thoughts. Only positive thoughts.

But seriously, I really wish the doctor on whom Mama's survival depends would remove his eyes from my sister's boobs and focus on his patient.

"How's she doing?" I ask.

Much to my relief, he slips back into professional-neurologist mode. "There's been no change."

My heart sinks. I was thinking— Oh, it's silly. I don't know what I was thinking—that, maybe while I was at the airport getting Summer, some sort of miracle would happen and she'd be awake when we got back? I give myself a mental shake. Being morose won't do Mama any good. We all need to remain *positive*. "I'm just sure it won't be long before she's awake and talking our ears off."

He nods, but the expression on his handsome face seems like he's humoring a silly child. Irritation flares inside me.

"It's been nearly forty-eight hours," I say. "Can't you give us a prognosis?"

"Comas are notoriously unpredictable. A person can be out for hours or years. There's really no way to know when or if a person will come out of one."

Summer goes pale. "Are you saying our mother might be like this for the rest of her life?"

Dr. Travis rubs his chin. "Unfortunately, that's a possibility, though not a probability. You see, brain injury severity is described using a scale of one to eight, with one being a deep coma and eight being a normally functioning uninjured person," he said. "Your mother is currently functioning at a level three, which means she's in a light coma. She can probably even be jostled awake by loud voices."

Summer frowns. "If she can be jostled awake, how come you can't just wake her up?"

He shrugs. "Therein lies the mystery of comas. Only time will tell. After that, it's anybody's guess. Let's go inside so you can see her."

We walk in and Summer gasps. "Oh, Ginny."

It's terrible to see her lying there black and blue and vulnerable, amidst the IV tubes and beeping, wheezing equipment. I know how hard this first glimpse of her is and I put a hand on Summer's shoulder. She doesn't pull away.

Ginny's eyelids flutter a bit and the sheet rustles as she moves her left foot.

I edge closer and touch her sheet-covered leg. "Mama? We're here. Summer and I are both here."

When she doesn't open her eyes, we turn to Dr. Travis, who is writing on her chart.

"Coma patients open their eyes sometimes, but it doesn't always mean they're awake. Such as what I mentioned earlier about voices rousing them."

"So what's next?" Summer demands.

"Depending on the severity of her head injury, we might need to get her into an inpatient rehabilitation center."

"A nursing home?" Oh, my Lord. The thought hitches my breath. I suppose it's better than the alternatives: Death. Or moving in with me. *Oh, how can I even think selfishly like that at a time like this?* Still, the thought of Mama in one of those places knocks me for a loop. At fifty-eight, she's too young for a nursing home. She has too much life left to live.

We hear the sheets rustle again and turn to see her

blinking at us, looking annoyed, as if we've interrupted her afternoon nap.

"I am *not* going to an old folk's home."

CHAPTER 3

Summer

Ginny's awake. Thank God.

"Mama?" Skye hurries to Ginny's bedside and grabs her hand. "Oh my goodness, we were all so worried. Look, Summer even flew down."

Skye gestures toward me, but Ginny's gaze skips over me, as if searching for someone else.

"Where's Jane?" she asks. "Is Jane here?"

A burning, metallic taste similar to the antiseptic smell of the hospital room creeps up the back of my throat. Suddenly, I'm eleven years old again. Small. Insignificant. A disappointment to my mother.

Skye darts a panicked glance at me, then at Dr. Travis, standing there as if he's watching a soap opera unfold. This irks me. Dammit, shouldn't he be doing *something*, especially given the cost of health care these days?

I move beside my sister. "Sorry, Ginny, Jane's not here. You're stuck with Skye and me." I can't keep the bitterness from my tone.

Skye nudges me and hisses. "Summer. *Shh*."

Thank God, the doctor finally comes to life. "Welcome back. Do you know where you are?"

Ginny squints at him as if she's trying to place him.

"I'm Dr. Travis and you're in Dahlia Springs Memorial Hospital. You were in a car accident. Do you remember anything?"

"Jane?"

"No, Mama, it's Skye and Summer."

She looks confused, gazing at us as if she can't quite place us. "I don't want you. I want my baby. I want my Jane."

I flinch. Her words are a punch to my gut. I'm a sucker, a fool for coming all the way down here against my better judgment. I hate myself for letting her get to me, letting her rejection matter.

God, I need a cigarette.

Skye clears her throat. I can actually see her regroup, straightening and plastering on that *I'm-in-*

charge-and-everything's-just-wonderful smile before she looks at Dr. Travis.

"Why don't you give us a few minutes?" He smiles. "In fact, go relax and have a cup of coffee while I examine her. By the time you finish, we should be ready for you."

For a moment I fear I'm slipping, that I might succumb to a dizzying spiral of emotion.

Skye touches my arm, and for some odd reason, that yanks me back from the brink. Oh, God. Not another panic attack.

"Mama, you just rest," she says. "We'll be back in a few minutes."

Ginny closes her eyes.

Dr. Travis walks us to the door. Despite my sister's all-is-well smile, I know Skye's just as flummoxed as I am because she's quiet. My sister is rarely quiet.

"Just give us fifteen minutes," he says before calling in his students so they can watch and listen. It reminds me of a carnival sideshow freakapalooza.

Step right up. See the woman who ate her young and hear the amazing story of how the children lived to tell about it.

Out in the hall, the air feels lighter. Free of the

essence of Jane that was crowding Ginny's room, edging us out. But I still have an annoying ringing in my ears.

Finally, Skye breaks the silence. "Well, how about that?" Her voice is low and conspiratorial.

"Yeah, how 'bout that. We're here, and only Jane will do. Some things never change."

She pushes the button on the elevator and crosses her arms. Her lips are pressed into a thin line and she's eyeing me with that disapproving-mother look.

"Actually, I was talking about our mother regaining consciousness."

Oh, get over yourself. This act might work on her kids, but I'll be dammed if she's going to make me feel like a schmuck. "Look, I'm glad Ginny is awake, but don't you get tired of the same old sorry song and dance? She wants Jane. You know where Jane is, so call her or go get her or *something*. Whatever it takes to make that woman happy. I certainly don't have it in me."

Skye sighs as if she's so exasperated she can't contain her disgust.

Fine. Whatever.

I turn my back on her and, with a shaky hand, pull out my cell phone and dial information. "Connect me to American Airlines, please."

"What are you doing?" Skye says the words to my back.

"Calling to change my flight."

She grabs my arm.

I pull out of her grasp.

The airline's automated attendant directs me to push the number two for reservations. As I do that, Skye walks around in front of me and stands there with her hands on her ample hips. "You can't leave. You just got here."

Oh, yeah? Watch me. I long to say the words, but my throat is closing up.

"How can you do this without even talking to the doctor? Summer, Mama may be awake, but we don't know for certain she's okay."

I turn away from her, tempted to stick my finger in my free ear, but the elevator dings and the doors open. I glance over my shoulder at the empty lift. "Go on," I manage to choke out. "I'll catch up with you in a minute."

No such luck. The doors slide shut without her.

"Reservations, how may I help you?" says a male voice on the other end of the line.

I draw in a deep breath, but it doesn't fill my lungs. "I need to change my return flight to the first available flight from Dahlia Springs Municipal to La-Guardia."

I give him my ticket information and feel a little steadier, since I was able to get the words out.

"Please hold and I'll check for you." I hear him typing on the other end of the line.

Skye glares at me, her chin jutting forward. "I *cannot* believe you're leaving…."

"I have a flight out of Dahlia Springs Municipal connecting in Atlanta—" Skye, with her ability to drown out the world when she wants to be heard, starts talking at the same time as the airline rep. I stick my finger in my ear and close my eyes to block her out.

"Would you repeat that?" I say. "It's noisy here."

"I can get you on a flight to LaGuardia by way of Atlanta at two p.m. Monday."

My eyes fly open. "I beg your pardon? This is Thursday." Skye lifts an eyebrow and smirks. I turn away from her. "I need to fly out sooner." Or I'll die.

I don't want to die in Dahlia Springs. "Why not today or tomorrow?" Tomorrow at the *very* latest. *Please*.

"The last American Airlines flight for this week left Dahlia Springs twenty-three minutes ago."

"So you're telling me there are no flights out of this place for four days?"

"Not on American. There's not a big demand for flights to Dahlia Springs so we only provide service Monday through Thursday."

Not a big demand. Surprise, surprise.

My heart pounds. I put my hand on my chest and take a deep breath to calm myself. "Oh, God. I'm stuck."

"Excuse me?" he says.

I rack my brain for a solution. "Can't you route me through a different city?"

More typing. My heart feels like it's keeping time with his keyboard cadence.

Skye's in my face again. "I *really* can't believe you." She puts her hands on her temples, like the drama queen she is. "No, wait, yes I can. It's just like you to hightail it when things are tough."

Oh. I'm tempted to slug her. My mouth is dry, but I manage to choke out, "Now you wait just a minute."

The airline rep says, "Certainly, I can hold."

"No, not you." My voice shakes. "You keep looking for a flight."

Typing resumes, and an orderly walks by pushing
a medicine cart. He's the first person I've seen
outside of the ICU. I'm tempted to ask him if he has
a spare Xanax in his rolling pharmacy.

Skye throws up her hands. "Go your merry way
and leave it all to me. You are undoubtedly the most
selfish woman I've ever known."

All I can think of as I watch her walk back to
the elevator and push the call button is, *No one
knows you like a sister. Unless your sister doesn't know
you at all.*

Mine's obviously never known me if she thinks
this is easy for me.

I put my hand over the mouthpiece. "No one's
asking you to stay, Skye."

She turns and blinks at me. "I will not leave
Mama like this."

"Yeah, well what about all those times Mama left
us?"

"That was different. You know it was."

I press my fingers to my forehead because my head

feels as if it's about to explode. "What the hell do you expect me to do? Stay here forever?"

The rep says, "I apologize, I'm working as fast as I can."

Oh, God. "And you're doing a great job," I say. "I was talking to my sister."

The elevator dings and Skye gets in. A wave of relief washes over me as the doors slide closed like a firewall between us.

"I have some alternatives for you," he says. "There's an eight-o'clock flight out of Orlando this evening or a seven-o'clock flight out of Tallahassee tomorrow morning."

Those are my choices? I take a deep breath and try to conjure some charm, but it can't cut through the mire of the panic attack that's been building since Ginny awakened. "Nothing else? Isn't there a smaller airport that's closer?"

"No ma'am, these are the closest cities."

"Considering it'll take me four hours to drive to either Tallahassee or Orlando and only five hours to drive to Atlanta where I could hop on a direct flight, those don't sound like very good *options*, do they? Besides, I'd have to rent a car—"

I clench my moist hand into a fist. My nails dig into my palm. *Why am I telling him this?*

"I do apologize, but that's the best I can do."

Well, it's not good enough. God, a typical man.

"I can book you on the Monday flight or perhaps you'd like to try another airline?"

I take a deep breath and try to quell the panic that's cresting inside me.

I lean against the wall. It isn't his fault I'm stuck. He can't manufacture a flight. I squeeze my eyes closed and let the anxiety flow, feeling I'm stuck in a tiny box with my mother and sister and Nick. I want to claw my way out. But I can't. After spending six hundred dollars on my ticket to fly here, I'm not prepared to fork out more money on a rental car, much less buy a new ticket if another airline has a flight out of here. At almost three hundred dollars, the train isn't an option either. I checked on it before I bought my plane ticket.

Yep, I'm stuck.

"Okay, switch me to Monday."

Grasping for a coping mechanism one of the dozen or so shrinks I've seen over the past two decades equipped me with, I rationalize that it's only four days, and I go outside for a smoke.

Four days.

And I'll have the consolation of knocking Skye off her self-righteous pedestal. After all, I'm staying through Monday. She doesn't need to know I can't afford any other escape route.

Four days.

How much mental torture can Skye and Ginny inflict on me in that short amount of time?

Oh dear God, help me.

CHAPTER 4

Skye

Downstairs in the hospital cafeteria, it smells like they're cooking up something Italian. My stomach growls, but a quick glance at my watch shows it's a little too early for dinner.

Mmm…smells like lasagna.

Or spaghetti with meat sauce.

I so wish I could be like those people who lose their appetites when they're stressed. But, oh no, not me. I'm an all-occasion eater: Food is a celebration when I'm happy; comfort when I'm sad; sweet revenge when I'm mad; and just plain ol' fun when I'm bored.

I can't understand those odd creatures who can take or leave food. Summer, for instance. It's probably because she smokes; they say nicotine dulls the taste buds. Now that I think about it, she's always been a finicky eater, never been all that interested in food. Just like she's never been all that interested in anything that doesn't directly benefit her.

Such as staying and helping me take care of Mama until she's on her feet.

I suppose stewing over Summer right now doesn't serve any purpose. But sometimes she makes me so mad I could just boil over. I don't know why I thought she'd change. Except that we are in the midst of a crisis with Mama's condition—granted she's improving, thank God in heaven—and it would be nice if for once she could think outside herself, put her selfishness on the shelf.

As I make my way through the serving line, the cakes, pies and puddings call to me. But I remind myself this is hospital-cafeteria food. It can't be worth spending the calories on. Although that doesn't stop me from hesitating in front of a piece of angel food cake topped with fresh strawberries and whipped cream.

I glance over my shoulder at the door. Summer's bound to join me any minute, after she finishes making her plans, and despite how tempting the cake looks, I'd rather go hungry than eat it in front of her. So I settle for pouring myself a cup of coffee, angry at myself for caring what she thinks.

As I'm about to hand my money to the young woman at the register, I say, "Is it too late to add something else?"

She smiles sweetly. "No, not at all."

I grab a king-size pack of peanut M&M's from the candy rack behind me. *Yes, they should hit the spot.*

Armed with coffee and candy, I make my way to a corner table to hide with my snack. There are only three people in addition to myself in the cafeteria—a man in scrubs hunched over a newspaper and an older couple. The woman looks weary, as if she hasn't slept in days. The man with her is probably her husband. I wonder who she's worried about. Her mother? Her child?

My heart tightens at the thought. Suddenly, I'm almost overwhelmed by how much I miss my three. No parent should ever go through the pain of losing a child.

I suppose, in a sense, Mama must feel as if she's lost Jane. It makes me wonder which is worse: losing a child to the streets or death?

I know, because I was nineteen when Jane was born.

Even though both Summer and I were out of the house, I shared Mama's pain each time Jane ran away. I lived in constant fear that she was going to turn up dead.

I tear open the yellow candy wrapper and pop a red candy in my mouth. The sweet/salty goodness is pure comfort.

I had kids of my own the first time she left and, I don't know, I guess something shifts in you once you give birth. A well of vulnerability opens and dredges up feelings you never knew you could have.

Maybe that's the reason I can forgive Ginny for waking up asking for Jane. Summer doesn't understand mother love.

I eat two more pieces of candy as I fish my phone out of my purse. My neighbor, Rose, should have the kids home by now, and I'm longing to hear their sweet angel voices.

I call but the line is busy. One of them must be online. Cameron and I have been slow to switch over to Internet that doesn't run through the phone lines because we don't want to give them carte blanche. With three of them between the ages of twelve and sixteen, they'd be on the phone and computer all the time. At least this way only one piece of technology can be in use at a time and they have to battle it out amongst themselves.

Since I can't talk to them, I ring my husband's cell phone thinking he should be out of court by now, but I get his voice mailbox.

"Hi, honey, it's me," I say. "I hope you and the kids are all getting along okay without me. Well, I have some great news—Mama regained consciousness today. The doctor is in with her now. I'll call you later after I talk to him. But it looks like things are on the upswing. Of course, I'll have to stay until I know she's in the clear, even though Summer's already making plans to go home, but Mama will need *someone*."

I hang up and eat more candy. He always forgets to turn his phone back on after he's been in court. I was just hoping that, since I was away and Mama was in such bad shape, he'd be more conscious of keeping the lines of communication open. But that's all right. Really, it is. I guess I miss him more than I realized.

I flip open the phone again and dial his office. "Good afternoon, this is Skye Woods. May I speak to Cameron, please?"

"Good afternoon, Mrs. Woods. I'm sorry, but he's

not in the office. He's been in court today. May I take a message?"

My heart sinks a little. I give myself a mental shake. It's only been two days since I talked to him. And he's a busy man. Working on a rather high-profile civil case and all. "Oh, no, thank you. I'll catch up with him later this evening."

Next, I dial his pager and punch in my cell number. When I'm done I shove a handful of M&M's in my mouth. As luck would have it, just as I start chewing, Summer walks into the cafeteria. As fast as I can, I shove the remains of the candy into my purse, and swallow some of the pieces whole, nearly choking in the process. The rough edges scrape the back of my throat as they go down.

As she reaches my table, I wash away the evidence with a gulp of hot coffee that makes my eyes water.

"What's the matter?" Summer asks.

"You smell like smoke."

She rolls her eyes. "Smoking cigarettes is not a crime, despite your thinking it should be."

What? She has no idea what I'm thinking. She never has. "Summer, I do not think it should be outlawed. That's ridiculous."

"Whatever." She glances around the cafeteria. "I think we can head back up. Surely the doctor's finished by now."

"Don't you want a cup of coffee?"

She shakes her head.

When we're on our way to the elevator I ask, "So when are you leaving?"

She levels me with her gaze.

I'm so tired of bickering with her. I was merely asking and not being judgmental or inflammatory. I open my mouth to tell her so, but she says, "Monday."

"You're staying until Monday?"

She nods.

So do I, but I stay quiet because she looks like a storm cloud ready to burst. I'm afraid that if I ask her what changed her mind after she seemed hell-bent on getting the heck out of Dodge, she'll turn into an angry tempest.

Instead, we walk in silence up to Mama's room, where Dr. Travis meets us in the hall.

"I am very happy to report that given the circumstances, your mother's doing remarkably well."

The news makes my pulse beat a little faster.

"That's fabulous. Isn't it, Summer?"

"Fabulous," she echoes.

"She's not showing any repercussions from the head trauma that caused the coma. I want to keep her overnight for observation. Tomorrow morning, I'll run some tests to make sure everything's okay. If it all checks out, I'll release her, possibly as early as tomorrow afternoon or early Saturday."

"Thank you, Doctor. This is exactly what we were praying you'd say."

I'm not sure he hears me, because he's gazing over my shoulder. I glance back and realize he's watching Summer, who is eyeing him back in that unsmiling, penetrating, Angelina Jolie–aloof way of hers.

As usual, she's sucked all the energy out of the room. She's not really flirting with him as much as she's emitting vibes that seem to say, *Yes, I'm hot and I know that you know I'm hot. Too bad for you.*

"So," I say, feeling I'm intruding on a private party. "I guess I'll just pop on in and see her. Are you coming, Summer?"

She turns her aloof gaze on me and arches an eyebrow. For a few seconds, I'm afraid she's going to fling some flippant belittling dig to prove she's the alpha female. But she surprises me when she simply nods and says, "Thank you for the good news, Doctor."

Ginny

Time has a way of retouching memories, blurring recollections into a soft focus so pretty you can just about frame them. Well, maybe you can only hang those portraits in the mind's eye, because no one else would see them from quite the perspective you do.

Over the years, I've learned that if you look deep enough into the past, beyond the yellowing snapshots of sweet smiles and contrived poses, you'll catch a fleeting glimpse of truth.

Truth is rarely pretty, but I've learned the hard way you're better off choosing it over beauty. Even if at first it has a bitter taste.

I haven't always chosen right. And I did a lot of dumb things when I was young.

Now that I'm older, I don't need anyone sugarcoating the truth. And the truth is, I was a bad mother to my twin girls. It's plain and simple as that. The image of me during those times is scarred into my mind. Some of the snapshots are dark and stained, and others are grainy and hard to look at, but I don't want them to go away. Because periodically, I take them out and look at them and remind myself of the monster I was.

I suppose I could argue that as a single parent, I did the best I could. That it was a struggle to make ends meet when the girls were growing up. Blah, blah, blah. That doesn't change a damn thing.

It's just too bad I didn't have the money I have now, which I came into the old-fashioned way—I married it. But times were different when the twins were young and my good fortune can be a sore spot with them, so we don't talk about it much. Not that I haven't offered to share. They're just too proud to take it.

Strange how money changes everything. If I weren't a strong person, it could take me on a real mind trip. But given what's happened to me—Chester dying, the accident, the choices I've made—even if I wasn't in my right mind back then, it's enough to make a gal reevaluate her entire life.

I know what I have to do, and I'm prepared to do it. In fact, if I have my way—and I usually do—not only will I make everything right with the twins, I'll finally bring my Jane home, too.

I just hope I don't lose all three of them in the process.

Summer

We push open the door to Ginny's room. She's lying with her eyes closed, the arm that isn't full of tubes and needles over her eyes.

Skye and I stand at the foot of her bed. Bruises mar her porcelain-doll face. She always reminded me of a blond Naomi Judd. So small and fragile looking. On the outside, that is. There's nothing fragile about Ginny on the inside. Still, despite everything, the sight of her bruised and battered makes me feel sick.

She opens her eyes.

"Mama?" says Skye.

I don't know what to say. So I don't say anything.

Ginny blinks at us, then smiles. "My precious angel twins. As I live and breathe." Her eyes well and a tear breaks free to meander down her cheek. "I was just thinking about y'all and here you are. Like magic." She holds out her hand to us and we move toward her, Skye first. I trail behind her.

"Mama, we're here." Skye takes her hand and I step up to the bed and put my hand on top of my sister's. It reminds me of that stupid game we used to play when we were kids—the one where everyone sticks in a hand, one on top of the other, and the person whose hand is on the bottom pulls it out and puts it on top and it keeps going until someone gets tired and quits.

Funny, the parallels—both Skye and me vying to be top of the heap, beating ourselves up to keep from getting stuck on the bottom. No wonder Jane divorced the lot of us.

Ginny eyes me up and down. "You're so skinny, girl. We'll have to fatten you up while you're here." She looks at Skye. "And you could stand to give a few pounds to your sister. Oh, but you're both beautiful. Both of you. My beautiful, beautiful babies."

My nerves are shot, and I can't look at my sister. I don't know how she's going to take Ginny's comment. I can't deal with any more drama.

Breathe in.

Breathe out.

"Where's Jane?" Ginny says. "Did she come, too?"

I blink, wondering if she remembers asking for her earlier. Surely not.

"No, but I know where she is. She's in Springvale, Mama," Skye says. "You got better so fast I didn't have a chance to get a hold of her."

Ginny closes her eyes, and her hand droops beneath ours. As Skye and I pull our hands away, Ginny's face contorts.

"I know I was a bad mother to you girls." She swipes away the tears flowing down her cheeks. "But I tried. Lord knows I tried. You have to know I did the best I could. Still, I know things weren't like they should've been, and I know I have no right to ask this of you, but I'm going to anyway."

She takes a deep breath. The exhale comes in ragged shudders. "Since y'all know where Jane is, will you take me to her? *Please?*"

Her eyes beseech us.

Skye and I look at each other. I can almost read my sister's thoughts because this is one of the rare occasions when she and I seem to be on the same page. I feel it.

"Mama, I'd be happy to call Jane for you." Skye

opens her purse, pulls out a notebook and flips to a phone number. "We can tell her what's happened, but—"

"No!" Ginny struggles to pull herself into a sitting position, but she eventually gives up and falls back into the bed. It's strange to see her like this.

"Please. No," she pleads. "Don't call her. She'll just run away. She'll disappear somewhere I can't find her. Please. I need my three girls all together."

Skye glances at me, then back at Ginny. "Mama—"

"There's things you need to know." Her voice raises a few notches. "Things you *must* know."

"Ginny, don't do this now. It can't be good for you. The doctor said you'll probably get to go home tomorrow, but if you get all worked up, it might set you back."

She turns her face toward the window, away from us.

"I don't know how to make you understand." Her voice is low and serious. "I could have died."

Skye touches her shoulder. "But you didn't. Mama, never once did we lose faith that you'd come out of this fine."

Mama silences her simply by holding up her hand. Just like she used to when we were children.

"I *am* going to die—someday. What I have to tell you cannot go with me to the grave." She swallows as if the words are stuck in her throat. "But first, I need Jane here. Because it concerns her as well as you. So please, I am begging you, my sweet babies. Please let's go get your sister. Let's all three bring Jane home. Please tell me you'll do it."

CHAPTER 5

Summer

The hospital staff move Ginny to a regular room since she's doing so much better. Skye and I stay until Raul arrives at the hospital and then we go to our mother's house to try and figure out what we're going to do. Or should I say try and figure out how we're going to get out of this road trip she's trying to rope us into.

As we pull up to the wrought-iron gate that surrounds the huge estate, the first thing I see is *Welcome to Hamby Hall* written in ornate script across the top of the gate. The ironwork alone probably cost as much as a small house.

Skye punches in the code as if she goes to Ginny's place every day. The gate swings open and she drives for what seems like miles up the brick driveway that's lined by gnarly coastal trees and lush north Florida vegetation.

This is the first time I've seen Ginny's house. I'd seen photos of it when she sent me the *Better Homes and Gardens* spread that ran in an issue shortly after construction was complete. She was so proud of the place—a sprawling, two-story number designed to look like a castle, complete with turrets and a front door that looks like a drawbridge. The place must be worth millions, even if it is a little out of place on a southeastern beach. My mother always has marched to her own tune.

"Mama did all right for herself, huh?" says Skye.

"Or should we say Chester Hamby did all right by Ginny?" I quip.

Skye shrugs and maneuvers the car under the port cochere.

The one and only time in Ginny's life that she got married was to Chester Hamby. They had been married for fourteen years when Chester died of a heart attack.

If you can get beyond the fact that he was twenty years older than she was and ugly as a troll, he was kind to my mother and the tale of how she hooked up with old Chester is kind of a Cinderella story.

Skye and I left home right after high-school graduation. She went to college at Florida State University and I left for New York to model. Ginny was working at Joe's Fountain over on Main and Dune. The way Ginny tells it is that Chester had just moved to Dahlia Springs from a town in the midwest—why he chose to move himself and his fortune to Dahlia Springs of all places is a mystery. There are many prettier beaches for a person with unlimited resources, but he moved here and soon he became one of Ginny's regulars at the diner. Three months later she called from Vegas to announce that she was pregnant and they were married. Skye was just as surprised as I.

Ginny was only thirty-seven. She'd waited this long to get married and the lucky guy was ugly, old Chester Hamby? She had this incredible, fragile beauty that men found irresistible—still does. She could've had any man she wanted if she'd just gotten the hell out of Dahlia Springs. But he adored her and he never asked questions. She told me he wasn't interested in her past. It didn't matter who or what she'd been before they met. All that mattered was that she loved him from that moment forward.

And she did.

He freed her from the diner, gave her financial security for the first time in her life, encouraged her to get involved in charity work (she started the Galloway-Hamby Foundation and over the years has become quite a philanthropist). He left her a wealthy woman when he died.

Who am I to argue with that? Death separated Chester and Ginny. He didn't walk out on her like Nick left me.

Nick....

I think about calling him, but it seems futile. What's the use of dredging up the past? Maybe Ginny has the right idea finding herself a gorgeous, young thing—

"Does Raul live here?" I ask.

Skye shakes her head. "Of course not."

I give her a knowing smile. "Oh, come on. She's not making the houseboy work overtime?"

Skye tries unsuccessfully to suppress a smile. I can almost see her biting the insides of her cheeks, but the smile wins, and I grin, too.

"I thought so, too, at first, but there's no trace of him in the house and she's still got all these photos of her and Chester all over the place. Don't you think Raul would be a little more... I don't know... *concerned* if they were involved? I just don't get that vibe from him."

We get out of the car, and I carry my bag inside. I park my suitcase in the cavernous foyer and look around. A huge mirror in a gilded frame hangs on the wall directly across from the front door. It must be at least seven feet tall by five feet wide. To my right is an open door. I can see into a formal dining room that looks like it might have been modeled after a king's dining hall.

"Let's go in the family room where it's more comfortable."

Family room? I didn't realize castles had family rooms. Skye ushers me into a space that's less formal. There are floral arrangements on nearly every surface.

"Look at all these flowers," I say.

"From Mama's admirers—charities and local businesses. She can't have them in ICU so they sent them here."

The room is elaborately decorated—a large, fashionably worn leather sectional is the centerpiece. A sturdy mahogany coffee table sits in front of it;

matching end tables with brass handles sit at each end. The largest television I've ever laid eyes on occupies the wall to my right. The east wall is all French doors out to a deck that overlooks the beach. The setup reminds me of a common area in an expensive resort. I wouldn't be surprised if Ginny had it designed that way on purpose.

It's a lot of house for one woman—and her boytoy. I walk over to the French doors and look out at the sea. It's high tide, and the water is lapping the shore in furious slaps. Despite how we struggled while Skye and I were growing up, I know I shouldn't begrudge Ginny a good standard of living or a young boyfriend. It's just a lot to digest all at once.

She offered to give me money once. It was after Chester died, and the estate was settled. Of course, I declined. I'm forty years old and I know better than to accept a handout from her. Anything from Ginny comes with a stipulation. As much as some extra cash would have helped, the price of getting tangled up in her web of manipulation was too high.

I scan the impeccably decorated room and something that looks out of place catches my eye. It's a display of cards on a shelf on the wall directly across from me.

Jane's birthday cards? Has to be.

I walk over and pick them up one by one. *Happy birthday to me!* inscribed in childlike script on the inside (Jane's writing)—and turning them each over to see the date, city and state printed meticulously on the back (Ginny's writing). It's always struck me as incredibly cheeky, Jane sending cards on her own birthday, especially when she never remembers Ginny's birthday. Still, our mother is always overcome to receive the cards. She calls Skye and me the moment she gets them and weeps with joy.

The first year Jane sent the card, she was still calling home every once in a while, but Ginny would get overwrought and demand Jane tell her where she was so Ginny could come get her. That's when Jane cut ties with her—except for the annual card. I must admit I always breathe my own sigh of relief because it means Jane's alive. Even if the postmark is the only clue to her life. But this year's card was postmarked Chicago. Hmm…

"Interesting you found her in Springvale." I finger the slick cardstock. "That's where Ginny was born and raised."

I glance at Skye, who's made herself at home on the couch. She's thumbing through an issue of *Better Homes and Gardens* that was on the coffee table.

"I know. I thought about that."

The thought of my little sister living in a homeless shelter floors me. I suppose the safety net in my mind's eye wouldn't let me imagine her anywhere worse than a succession of small, cheap, rent-by-the-week apartments. I'm sickened by the thought of her in a shelter with the lice and the smell of unwashed bodies. I shudder and want to beat myself up for letting her sink to this depth.

But how do you help someone who refused all your earlier attempts of help beyond free-flowing cash?

"You never told me how you found Jane. Did you hire a private investigator?"

Skye shrugs but doesn't look up from the article she's perusing. "You know I have lots of resources through Cameron's firm."

"If you had to pay anything, I want to contribute."

Skye tosses the magazine back on the coffee table. "Don't be silly. I didn't have any expenses."

The subtext is, *I wouldn't tell you if I did*, but I let it go.

"So what are we going to do about this road trip Ginny wants us to take?"

Skye bites her bottom lip and picks at her cuticle. "I don't know. With you leaving on Monday I just don't see how we can do it. I'm certainly not going with her by myself."

I put the card back in its place on the shelf, walk over to the sofa and sit down on the section across from her. I'm surprised how calm she is talking about it, given her dramatics when I tried to change my flight today. Then again, that was before Ginny started talking road trip.

"I'll have to discuss it with Cameron. A neighbor's minding the children while I'm gone. I told her it would only be a few days. I don't want to take advantage…"

Her voice trails off, and we sit in silence. Then she shrugs again. "Raul left us a note."

She picks up a piece of paper I hadn't noticed on the coffee table and hands it to me.

Good evening, ladies. Please make yourselves at home. Upstairs, I had the second room on the left made ready for Summer. If you're hungry, I ordered a lasagna and salad for your dinner. Please help yourselves to that and anything else you desire.

"Why don't you take your stuff upstairs? Get settled in and freshen up," she says. "I'll get dinner on the table."

I carry my suitcase up the marble staircase. My footsteps echo, and despite its grandeur, the big house feels empty. Maybe I'm just tired. It's been a long, emotional day.

At the top of the stairs, I turn right down a long hallway and, as I head toward the second room on the left, I notice a grouping of large photographs hanging on the wall a few feet down.

I stash my suitcase inside the bedroom Raul readied for me. It's large and beautiful, with a king-size bed with a gossamer canopy. The space is decorated in white and gold—white carpet, white furniture, white fabric with gold accents scattered here and there. It looks like a page out of *Architectural Digest*. But I am drawn to the photos grouped down the hall. The first cluster is an arrangement of Ginny and Chester kissing; Ginny and Chester raising a toast to each other; Ginny and Chester wrapping their arms around each other.

On the wall directly across from the Chester collection hang four photos—one each of Skye, Jane and me. And a fourth picture—the three of us with Ginny. It was taken in Tallahassee right after Skye's third child, Cole, was born.

Jane was young. Probably nine or ten because Nick and I were still married when I made that trip. Of course, he didn't come with me. He was probably away on a photo shoot or came up with some other convenient excuse to stay away.

I run my finger along the edge of the silver frame. It may be the only photo of the four of us together. We're all smiling. If someone didn't know better, they might think we looked…happy?

I walk down the hall, opening doors and peering in until I come to Jane's room. It looks as if Ginny left it untouched since the last time Jane walked out. Rock-and-roll posters on the walls, hot-pink carpet that must have been a special order, a fuzzy black duvet over a queen-size bed, little piles of clutter on every surface. I'm tempted to go in and sift through the remnants of my little sister's life to see if I can find clues that point to why she's chosen to live the way she has. Why she'd opt for a homeless shelter over a castle, but then images of the monster Ginny can be explode in my brain. I shut the door against the room's aura of sadness and walk away.

Still, Ginny seemed better with Jane than she was with us. Knowing what we lived with, how we lived, it was hard to watch Jane take everything Ginny gave her for granted. It was hard not to ask, "Do you know how good you have it?" After cutting ties with Ginny, Jane used to call Skye and me collect every once in a while. It was so hard talking to her and promising her we wouldn't tell Ginny because we knew Ginny was heartbroken over how Jane turned out.

Skye could afford to sneak Jane a few bucks here and there, but I wasn't making much money. I could barely afford to make ends meet to support myself. More important, we were afraid Jane was using the money to buy drugs. We agreed the handouts had to stop unless there was some accountability.

Jane wanted nothing to do with that.

So Skye and I agreed we had to practice tough love and cut off the cash. I tried to give Jane the benefit of the doubt for as long as I could. Because *I know* that dreams don't always work out the way you think they will. Jane set off to work with her boy-friend's band. The band broke up. The boyfriend dumped her and left her stranded. She was chasing a dream, and the dream crashed and burned.

This is one area in which Jane and I are more alike than my twin and I are. So who am I to judge? My life isn't exactly what I envisioned for myself when I was Jane's age. I took off for New York in the summer of 1984 with aspirations of becoming the next Paulina Porizkova. And here I am, a divorced human mannequin with no benefits, no job security and no more dreams. Because dreams don't always pan out. And unless you're stronger than the evil forces that prey on you, dreams get heavy. So heavy they can break your wings, drag you down and wash you out to sea.

That's why I tried time and time again to get Jane to come live with me, to get a job even if it meant waitressing or working retail until she'd saved enough to get on her feet. But Jane refused. Finally, she quit calling and disappeared. Except for the postmark on the envelope.

So, yes, I guess I wait just as anxiously as Ginny

does for the annual birthday card and each year come July, when Ginny informs us she's heard from Jane, we all breathe a collective sigh of relief and continue to live and let live.

After dinner I tell Skye I'm going for a run. I need a smoke, but I don't tell her that.

"Raul's lasagna was delicious," I say, "but I need to move this body before all that pasta and cheese take up permanent residence on my hips. Do you want to come?"

I don't know why I ask. The truth is, I'm going stir-crazy. I need some time alone to think. I need to get out of the house before I climb the walls.

"Go ahead. I'll do the dishes. I don't want to leave the mess for Raul."

I wonder if she's trying to make me feel guilty, or if it's just a noble excuse to get out of exercising?

"Besides," she adds, "I need to call Cameron and the kids to say good-night. I haven't had a chance to talk to him today and tell him the good news about Mama. Doesn't smoking make it hard for you to run without getting winded?"

Her non sequitur jars me, makes me whip my head around to look at her as I set my plate on the counter near the sink. "No more than being a couch potato would."

She gives me a look and starts drawing water in the sink.

She started it.

I excuse myself and go upstairs to change into running clothes and sneakers before more verbal barbs fly. It's only six-thirty, so it's still light out. I set out in the direction of downtown, astounded by how everything still looks the same after all these years.

I pass city hall, the post office, the town square and make my way south toward Mill Road. Before I know it, I'm standing in front of Nick's house.

The place belonged to his Uncle Byron for as long as we lived in Dahlia Springs. Byron raised Nick. His mother was a drug addict and wanted nothing to do with him, and his father cared even less. I suppose that was one of the reasons Nick and I bonded so deeply, why he and I worked and he and Skye didn't. We came from the same stock and weren't afraid to admit it. Skye, on the other hand, was proud and did everything in her power to paint a different picture of her life. There's nothing wrong with that, I suppose. Just different ways of thinking.

Byron succumbed to liver problems (read: he drank himself to death) a year after Nick and I divorced. He left the place to Nick.

The old house, which sits in the midst of a residential neighborhood, looks good. He's painted it a cheery yellow. The yard is neatly landscaped. It never looked this good when we were growing up. It's hard to reconcile.

I stand there and debate with myself whether I should go up and knock on the door. What's the harm in a friend who's in town for a short time stopping by and saying "Hi? He said he wanted to see me."

But it's gauche to stop by unannounced. Maybe I should go to a phone and call—

A motorcycle pulls into the driveway. A tall, lanky man unfolds himself from the bike and pulls off his helmet.

I freeze. Every nerve in my body stands on end. It's Nick, right there, silhouetted by the setting sun. I shade my eyes from the glare to get a better look.

"Summer? Is that you?"

He takes a few steps toward me, and I can't tell if he's happy to see me or not. Probably surprised, since it's been so long.

"Hi," I say. "I was passing through the neighbor-hood and I thought I'd say…hi."

That sounded stupid.

He smiles that crooked half smile that used to always do me in. Judging from the way my stomach does a triple-gainer, he can still work his magic. Damn him.

"It must have been a hell of a jog if you're in the neighborhood."

I shrug. He looks a little like Patrick Dempsey, only bigger and taller. Even after all these years, he still has the same brooding, dangerous air as when he followed me up to New York after Skye went off to college at Florida State.

Okay, I confess Skye found him first. They went to the prom or something equally banal. It's a long, complicated story. But it's not like I purposely plotted to steal my sister's boyfriend—although the way she tells it, it sounds like I systematically formu-lated a plan to abscond with her fiancé.

A big yellow Lab races across the street and jumps up on Nick, who catches him by the collar. "Hi, Jimmy, did you get out again?" he asks the dog, then turns to me and winks. "Jimmy comes out to greet me at least once a day." He gestures to the small brown bungalow across the street. "In about fifteen seconds Mrs. Lowenstein will appear and yell for Jimmy." Holding the dog by the collar, Nick checks his watch. "Just watch."

The words barely pass his lips when the front door across the street swings open. A frail, elderly woman sticks her head out and calls, "Jimmy? Where are you? Here, Jimmy! Oh, Nicholas is that you?"

She looks like a turtle sticking her head out of her shell as she cranes her neck to peer across the street. "Have you seen Jimmy? He seems to have gotten out again."

"Hi, Mrs. Lowenstein. Jimmy's right here. I've got him."

He smiles at me and under his breath he says, "We do this routine regularly. I'm going to go take Jimmy home. I'll be right back. Don't leave." My stomach pitches at the instant chemistry sparking between us. As if *divorce* and *eight years of separation* are words that don't apply to us.

To compensate for the rush of feelings swelling inside me, I whistle so that only he can hear me, and whisper, "Nick's got a girlfriend."

He laughs and lets Jimmy pull him across the street.

As he makes his approach, Mrs. Lowenstein shuffles out onto the porch. Her thin, unnaturally red hair is teased into a helmetlike coiffure. She's dressed in neat black slacks and a bright red blouse adorned with several long strands of gold chains and black beads the same color as her earrings. From my post on the sidewalk, I can see the slash of scarlet lipstick on her mouth. When she shuffles her way onto the top porch step, I notice the white scuffs on her feet. I smile at the thought of her dressing up for him.

Nick leads Jimmy, who is doing his best to jump up and lick him, in an awkward dance up the porch steps. I wonder how such a little woman can handle such a boisterous animal nearly as big as she is? But she yells out a hefty, "Sit, Jimmy," and I quit worrying about her.

Yes, Nick has always had this effect on women. Including my sister—no matter how short-lived that *association*... I wouldn't even go so far as to call it a *relationship*.

The short version is Skye and Nick had something like two dates. He came up to New York (where I happened to be living) to pursue his photography, and we fell in love.

We lived together for ten years. And it was heaven. But then he started pressuring me about marriage and babies.

God, I loved him. With my soul. But I didn't understand why we had to fix something that wasn't broken. He said it was because he'd decided he wanted kids by the time he was thirty.

I was like, whoa! Wait a minute. Rewind.

Kids were never part of the plan. At least not my plan. I would be a worse mother than Ginny was and I would never do that to a child.

I was flummoxed that children figured into his plan. At that point he'd been working for *Geographic International* for five years. He traveled a lot and seemed happy with our life together.

At twenty-seven, Gerard Geandeau had just opened his design salon. I was his favorite model. He was featuring me in print ads and outfitting me in his showpieces for the runway.

I didn't understand why Nick wanted to complicate things. Our careers were thriving, and he was talking about getting married and moving out of New York? Tying me down with a family while he traveled all over the world shooting for *Geographic International?*

Can you see the flaw in that picture?

All right, I admit, relationships are all about compromise. I thought I was meeting him halfway when I agreed to marry him. God, he was worse than a woman needing commitment. But we agreed there would be no kids. That was supposed to be his half of the compromise.

After we'd been married four years he realized I wasn't enough family for him. He never said that, of course. Not in so many words. Just packed his things and moved out.

This is only the second time since we signed the divorce papers that we've talked. I called him when Byron died. But talking to him was too hard. I still loved him. And then he got married and had the kid he was so desperate for.

Mama called me when she read about his wife's accident a year ago. I didn't know what to say so I sent him a card.

So here I stand, heart pounding and tongue-tied,

wishing like hell I hadn't decided to run, because I must look like death and smell even worse.

Mrs. Lowenstein gives Nick a peck on the cheek. As he crosses the street, I try to think of something intelligent to say, but all my mind can register is how fine he looks in his faded jeans and black T-shirt.

The visual sucks the breath right out of me. So all I can do is stand there mute, trying to figure out what it is about him that does this to me.

His broad shoulders? His gorgeous face (not too pretty, not too rugged)? Or maybe it's that cocksure way of his that's just this side of arrogant.

"You look…hot," he says.

My heart does a backflip, and I quirk an eyebrow at him. Hot? Hot's good. Very good.

"This humidity's a killer," he says. "You'd better come inside for some water so you can cool off."

Oh. Not hot as in *hot*. Hot as in sweaty and smelly.

"Or if you'd rather have a glass of wine or… something."

Hmm, so we're progressing from water to wine. "Or something? What exactly did you have in mind?"

Before he can answer, the screen door bangs

open and a little boy comes running out. "Daddy! You're home!"

Daddy? Oh, God.

The child runs up, attaches himself to Nick's leg like Velcro and stares up at me. I see the devil in his sparkling brown eyes.

Nick's eyes.

I'm not good when it comes to guessing a kid's age, but he looks like he's probably younger than five. So young to be without a mother.

A pretty blonde who looks to be in her twenties bangs the screen door open just like the boy did. The sound makes me flinch. "I told you never to go outside without telling me first," she calls. It's not a mean yell. Not like how Ginny used to scream at us so the whole neighborhood could hear her. It's a yell that falls somewhere between amused and exasperated.

I take a step backward away from Nick, and look at him and the boy and the woman who is walking toward us, smiling, looking way too perky and young.

His girlfriend?

If so, I don't want to meet her. "Oh, well, I should

have called first. I don't want to barge in. Really. I'd better go."

Nick reaches out and takes my hand. "Don't go. I want you to meet Jordan."

CHAPTER 6

Skye

One of the things I love about housework is that it frees your mind. I've solved some of my biggest dilemmas over a sink of hot water and frothy suds. There's something meditative about it that washes away the mind's clutter. I need to sort out what I want to do about this road trip before I talk to Cameron.

That's one of the reasons I opted out of jogging with Summer. Well, that and the fact that I hate jogging. So now that Mama wants us to go get Jane, what do we do? I mean Jane doesn't want to be found. If we go, what are we going to do once we get to her?

It just doesn't feel right.

I plunge my hands into the water, close my eyes and, as I pluck a glass from the suds and wash it, I search deep in my soul to see if I'm really concerned about respecting Jane's wishes or if I'm just afraid that if we go, Mama and Summer will find out that I didn't hire a private investigator to find Jane.

I didn't have to.

I've known all along where she's been living these past five years. Every time she moves she calls me and tells me where she is, even if she doesn't share much else about her life. I don't pressure her, because I saw how fast she cut off Mama and Summer when they did.

I've been sending her money to make sure she has food in her stomach. Cameron doesn't even know. I take it out of my "mad money." It's not very much. Oh, maybe a hundred dollars a month or so. More when I can swing it.

I couldn't just cut her off. I figure I have so many blessings, Jane needs the money more than I do.

I pull a plate out of the soapy water and give it a good scrubbing. Mama would never forgive me for not telling her I've known Jane's whereabouts, and Summer would be furious that I violated our agreement to quit giving her handouts. But I know Summer couldn't afford to keep shelling out the money.

I rinse the plate and it's as I'm drying it to a shine that I decide some things are better kept as secrets.

I pull out another plate and scrub at the dried tomato sauce. Besides, the thought of being confined in a car for several days with Mama brimming over with the need to confess makes me want to contemplate hara-kiri.

I don't know what she has to say, but I'm sure I don't want to hear it. I mean she's never been compelled to share her secrets before. I think this knock on the head has jarred something loose. Maybe if we just go on about our business like we always do—no road trips or excessive togetherness—whatever she knocked loose will settle back into place. It kind of reminds me of when I was in college and one of my sorority sisters imbibed a little too zealously. The A number one rule was friends don't let friends drink and dial. Because they always ended up calling a boy and saying things they'd never say had they been in their right mind.

I am going to apply the same principle with Mama. She's obviously not in her right mind if she wants to share with Summer and me.

As I move on to the silverware, it strikes me that her I-have-secrets-to-spill routine might just be a way to manipulate us into doing what she wants. Mama is a master manipulator and it wouldn't surprise me at all if she had nothing substantial to say except *thanks for the ride, it's been fun!*

That's probably it. Really, if I think about it, it's vintage Mama. How do I explain this? She's like a ride on the Tilt-A-Whirl. Whipping you this way and that whether you want to go this way and that or not.

No, actually, the Tilt-A-Whirl is too tame. Mama is a wild ride with no seat belts that sometimes leaves you hanging upside down while she changes direction to do something else—like enlist the rescue squad for help with a hangnail. Mama is all about the drama and I am not about to get suckered into her scheme of driving halfway across the U.S. because she wants to bring Jane home.

It's almost eight o'clock when I finish washing dishes. As I sit down to phone my husband, I'm a little miffed because I thought he would've returned my call by now. He probably never turned his cell phone on. But surely he would have gotten the message from his secretary.

It rings eight times before Becky, my sixteen-year-old answers. "Hello?"

"Becky, honey, it's Mama. Are you on the other line?"

"Yeah."

"Oh, I see. Well, you'll have to call whoever it is back because I need to talk to your daddy."

"I'm right in the middle of something important—"

"I don't care if you're talking to the Queen of England, young lady. I have good news about your grandma and I need to talk to daddy."

She makes a snorting sound that reminds me of Summer's insolent manners. "Like I would ever want to talk to the Queen of England." In my mind, I can almost see her rolling her eyes.

"I don't like your tone of voice, missy. Just because I'm not there doesn't mean I can't ground you, and I will if you don't put your father on the phone this instant."

"Fine. At least let me tell Darrin I'll call him back."

I should have known she was talking to a boy.

"Fine. But if it takes longer than one minute, you're grounded. And I'm not kidding. I'm timing you. Starting now."

I hear a thud like she's dropped the phone, then I hear her voice.

"My mother is such a loser. I have to hang up so she can talk to my father."

It only takes a split second to realize she thought she was talking to that boy. Heat washes over my cheeks and my body goes numb. *She called me a loser.* The line obviously didn't click over and she thought she was talking to—in another split second, anger floods my entire being.

"This *is* your mother, Rebecca. And you are grounded. Put your father on the line *now*. Darwin will just have to figure out on his own that you're not coming back on the line and you won't be for a very long while."

"God, mom! His name is name is Darrin, not Darwin."

"I don't care what his name is. Get your father. Now!"

She mutters something under her breath, and I think I hear the words *fat* and *loser*.

"Rebecca Woods! What did you just say?"

But the phone clunks in my ear as if she's slammed it against the counter, and I hear her yelling, "Dad! Mom's on the phone."

I wait, hoping one of my other two children will

pick up. I hear a TV blaring in the background and in my head I hear Becky calling me a loser. My own daughter. It's so nice to know I'm missed.

Numbly, I walk to the refrigerator and take out the dish of raspberry cobbler that Raul left for dessert. I heat a good-size portion in the microwave and top it with a big scoop of vanilla ice cream. It's the all-natural kind with the bits of vanilla bean I like so much.

By the time Cameron answers I'm halfway through dessert, and I'm so mad at my daughter and my husband it's a wonder I haven't sprouted horns and fangs. I probably would have if not for the pie. Maybe I'll have another piece when I get off the phone—

"Hello?" He sounds mildly irritated.

"Cameron? What took you so long?"

"I was going to the bathroom, Skye."

"Oh." The spoon clatters as I set it in the dish. "Well, I'm sorry to disturb you. I need to talk to you and I've been trying to reach you all day. Did you get my messages?"

He sighs. "I was in court all day. I had my phone turned off."

"Well, it's after eight o'clock. You're certainly not

in court now. I left you a message at the office, too. Didn't you get that one? I told your secretary it was urgent for you to call me as soon as possible."

Okay, so maybe I'm exaggerating a little bit, but I want him to feel guilty.

"I didn't go back to the office." His voice is prickly. "I had to pick up Sydney and Cole. Rose backed out at the last minute. Migraine or something. What's the matter? Is everything okay with your mother?"

This is selfish—because, *really*, I am so glad Mama's okay—but a teeny-tiny part of me wishes I had something tragic to slap him with.

"Mama woke up today."

"Well, that's wonderful news, Skye. Give her my best."

His best? I'm tempted to ask him to define what he means by *his best*, because the last time I checked, he didn't even like Mama.

He tolerates her. We live a safe four hours away from her so that's easy to do. We see her on the obligatory holidays: Thanksgiving or Christmas. One or the other, but not both because whichever holiday we spend with her, we spend the other with my country-club-dwelling in-laws. The two sets of parents don't mix.

"All right, then I'll see you tomorrow," he says.

"Wait a minute. Don't hang up. What are Sydney and Cole doing?"

"They're watching TV. They finished their homework, and I'm letting them have some downtime."

"They're not watching MTV, are they?"

"I have no idea what they're watching."

"Well, why don't you go in there and check, Cameron, because most of the stuff on MTV is not appropriate for twelve- and thirteen-year-olds."

He heaves a sigh, and I want to say, *See, being a stay-at-home mom isn't as easy as it seems, is it?* But I don't.

Instead, I listen as Cameron carries the phone into the family room, trying to identify the show my children are watching.

"What show is this?" His voice is flat.

"*Real World,*" says my twelve-year-old, Sydney.

The Real World?

"They're fine, it's just *The Real World.*"

"Cameron, *The Real World* is not fine. That's what they're *not* supposed to be watching."

"You said MTV."

"*The Real World* is on MTV and it is *not* appropriate. They have sex on that show." It's all I can do to keep from screaming at him.

"Well, isn't watching people have sex better than watching people kill each other?" I cringe because I can't believe he's talking about that in front of the children, but I know if I call him on it he'll just make a bigger issue of it in front of them.

"Cameron, you are completely missing the point. They know they're not supposed to watch that show and I am furious that they'd take advantage of the situation while I'm away. Tell them to turn it off and that I will deal with them when I get home."

"Oh, for God's sake, Skye."

"Cameron, just do it, please!"

"Kids, your mother says turn off the television and she will deal with you when she gets home." His monotone voice nearly sends me through the roof.

Muted protests spike in the background, but soon the sound of the television dies and the room falls silent.

"There. Thank you. That's better. Now may I speak to them? I'd like to say good-night."

"Look, Skye, they just went upstairs. They're a

little mad at you right now. Why don't you just leave them alone? When are you coming home?"

Just leave them alone? His words slap me. I know it's childish, but it hurts my feelings. My oldest calls me a loser and Sydney and Cole are mad because I caught them doing something they know darn well they're not supposed to be doing…and I should just leave them alone? I haven't talked to them in two days. I take a deep breath to steady myself.

I knew the teenage years would be hard, but I don't think it's unreasonable to expect my children to show me a little respect. To miss me a little when I go away?

If I were ever tempted to cry it would be now. But I won't. I don't cry. Can't remember the last time that happened.

I swallow hard to make sure the tears don't break the surface. I push them back down, deep in the hidden spring that drifts at the base of my soul, that internal river of tears that's been streaming constantly for as far back as I can remember. No matter what happens in life, my inner levy never breaks.

The water level recedes and once again, the

spring flows silently within. It's somewhat of a touch-stone. Despite all the turmoil of late, at least one thing in my life remains constant: I do not cry.

A hateful voice deep down inside me bubbles up and says, *They don't need you anymore.*

I know it's true. They don't need me like they used to. And it's not a bad thing, either. That's basic child psychology. It's all part of the process. Healthy children grow up and leave home. I should be happy about them budding into fine young adults because that means I've done my job well.

I have a fast-forward vision of myself in ten years, the displaced homemaker who has no purpose in life since her kids moved on. Cameron still has his career, but what am I left with? A sick chill works its way through me and I have to take a deep breath to ward it off.

"Skye, are you there? I asked when you're coming home."

"I don't know when I'm coming home, Camer-on." The words spill from my mouth. My insides clench, and I can't believe what I'm saying. "Mama's coming home from the hospital tomorrow, but she needs me to do something for her. I'll probably be gone another week. Ten days, maybe. You'll just have to get along without me."

He sighs again. "Skye. Is this a joke? You can't be gone ten days. You're needed here. I have a heavy court load over the next couple of weeks and I can't take off work like I did today."

The stupid thing is my heart responds to the part, *you're needed here*. But he doesn't say *he* needs me or the children *want* their mama. Or that anyone wants *me* to come home. I know it's semantics, but he's a lawyer. He's good with twisting his words around to get what he wants. He's not even trying to finesse it with a fresh coat of paint or a pretty ribbon.

I'm needed. Like the checkout clerk in the market needs the bagger. To facilitate. To make life easier.

"Rebecca can help out," I say. "She's sixteen years old." I remember I haven't told him she's grounded, but even as mad as I am, I don't want to end our conversation on that note.

"Skye, look, Virginia can afford to hire an entire fleet of live-in nurses. Why are you letting her manipulate you like this?"

I want to laugh out loud. *Who is trying to manipulate whom, Cameron?*

"Let Virginia get someone else to do her bidding. Come home."

There's a click. The line falls silent.

No *I love you*. No *I miss you*.

Just ugly, dead silence.

CHAPTER 7

Summer

I stand on the sidewalk in front of Nick's house and try to smile at the perky blonde and the little boy clinging to his leg. But my facial muscles weigh a ton.

Figures Miss Perky—Jordan—would have one of those great androgynous names. That's so of her generation—a generation that could very well make her Nick Russo's daughter. I really can't believe he'd stoop so low as to hook up with someone so young.

You old goat.

Sexy old goat.

Just you wait, Jordan, when he's sixty and downing Viagra like candy to keep up with you because you'll only be forty—the prime of your life.

Oh, God. I'm forty and if this is prime time...

The ringing starts in my ears and my heart pounds like the bongo player I saw in the Village the other day.

I'm caged.

Trapped.

Can't breathe.

God, two anxiety attacks in one day. That's why I didn't want to come back to Dahlia Springs. That's why it was a stupid idea to run by Nick's house.

"Summer, this is my son, Jordan."

Inhale—I blink. Jordan's his son? Oh.

I manage to offer the boy my hand. He shakes it. "Jordan, this is Summer." First name only, I notice. I wonder how much Nick's told Miss Perky about me. Isn't this cozy.

"I'm five," says the boy.

I nod, unable to force words through the cobwebs in my throat.

"This is Tammy," Nick says. "She's Jordan's baby-sitter."

"*Oh.*" I swallow hard and hope my blurt didn't sound the way I think it did.

"Nice to meet you, ma'am."

She has such a thick Southern accent that it doesn't even matter that she's just called me *ma'am*.

Or maybe it's that she's Tammy, the babysitter. Not Nick's girlfriend.

The thought is so absurd, I notice with relief that my panic is subsiding, like high tide slowly ebbing away. I take a deep breath just to be sure, and the air almost fills my lungs to the bottom.

Good. It's all good. So, Nick's moved on. This is his son. Knowing he had a son and seeing him are two different things. Still, it's all good. And it helps that he doesn't explain who I am. Because it's complicated. It is. How do you explain to a little boy that his father had another life with another woman long before the child was born? I don't really want to go there and it's plain to see he doesn't, either.

"Tammy, Jordan, it was nice to meet you. Nick, always good to see you. I have to run. Ha. Literally."

Shit. I'm rambling. I step to the side. The next thing I know my ankle buckles and I'm falling in a freakish, distorted slow motion, skinning my elbow and landing hard on my right hip.

Nick and Tammy gasp and scramble to help me. I try to prove I'm fine by hopping up fast, but I stumble like a graceless, uncoordinated cow. My foot throbs. Shifting my weight to my good leg, I strike a nonchalant pose because I just want to get the hell out of here.

"Summer, God, I'm sorry. The damn sidewalk is uneven. The roots from that old oak are breaking through. I've called the city three times to get them out here to fix it, but they haven't gotten to it yet. That really pisses me off."

I glance down at a three-inch step up from one block of concrete to the next. The gnarly fingers of tree root are barely visible, but sure enough, that's what's pushing up the walk.

He's called the city. Nick's concerned about the state of his sidewalk. This is not the man I used to know. That man lived in an apartment in the city where the only thing he had to worry about where side-walks were concerned was not stepping in dog poop.

"Can you walk?" Nick asks.

"Sure. I'm fine." I take a step and icy-hot pain shoots up my shin. "Ahh."

Nick runs his hand over the stubble on his cheeks. "Here, let me help you." He slips his arm around my waist, and I cringe because I'm sure I stink, but *ahh*, what choice do I have if I want to walk?

"Tammy, will you go in and fix a bag of ice?"

She nods. "Come on, buddy," she says to Jordan. "Come in and help me get Miss Summer some ice."

From *ma'am* to *miss* in the span of one fall. That's such a Southernism, calling everyone miss whether they're young or old, married or single. *Miss Summer. Miss Tammy.*

"Let's get you inside so I can check and see if anything is broken."

As Nick's side presses against mine the familiar feel and smell of him—soap and leather and something green—rushes back to me. Despite the pain, I lean into him, savoring his nearness.

I'm tall—five ten—and one of the things I always loved about him was his height. He made me feel small and feminine. There are other things about him that I love—err…loved—we just worked. Together. Nick and I. I really thought we were soul mates until that baby issue tore us apart. It got to be a stand off. If he really loved me, I should have been enough for him. And we know how that turned out.

He settles me on the living-room couch and props my leg up on sofa pillows. All I can think is I'm so glad I shaved my legs this morning.

Well, that's not my only thought. As Jordan

hands Nick the ice Tammy's wrapped in a kitchen towel, I'm thinking Nick is a good father. I can tell in the few minutes I've been around them. He was right to leave me for not wanting to give him a child. In that instant, my heart breaks all over again.

"Does it hurt?" Nick asks. His question almost makes me weep—that is, until he moves my foot and the shooting pain makes me cry out.

"Yes! Ouch! It hurts."

Jordan runs to Tammy and buries his face in her skirt. "Come on, buddy, let's go into the kitchen and play a game." She ushers him into the other room.

See, I would have been a bad mother. I scare children.

Nick puts the ice on my foot, his dark eyes gazing intently into mine. "That's a good sign because it probably means it's not broken, but I still think you should get an X-ray."

I shake my head. "No, I can't."

"Why not?" he asks. "If you don't have insurance, I'll pay for it. Because you don't, do you?"

It irks me how well he still knows me. Wasn't it part of the divorce settlement that he relinquish all intimate knowledge of what makes me tick?

"I don't have time." He's looking at me as if he's waiting for me to explain what could be so urgent. For lack of anything better, I say, "I'm supposed to take Ginny somewhere."

His brows slide together. "Tonight? Can't it wait until morning?"

"We're supposed to leave in the morning. I just—"

"Well, come on. Let's get to the hospital then."

I rest my head on the back of the couch, frustrated because, just like old times, I never could say no to this man. Except when it came to the things that mattered.

"Tammy?" he calls. "Can you stay a little later? I'm going to take Summer in for an X-ray to make sure nothing's broken."

She walks to the archway between the kitchen and the living room. "No problem."

I catch a glimpse of something in her eyes as she gazes at him. Something that tells me she's smitten with her handsome employer.

"Thanks," he murmurs. "We shouldn't be too long, but if I see we're going to be, I'll call." His words are so to the point I don't think the feeling is mutual. At least I hope not. Nick was a lot of things—stubborn, hotheaded, passionate, charming—but he wasn't a flirt.

"Do you need to call Ginny?" he asks.

Busted.

"No." I take a deep breath, feeling stupid for using her as an excuse to get out of the x-ray. "Ginny's in the hospital."

"Why? What's wrong?"

I wave him off. "It's a long story. I'll tell you on the way to the hospital. But I should call Skye. She's at Ginny's house."

Nick stiffens. "She's here, too?" But before I have a chance to answer he says, "Because of Ginny, right?"

I nod.

"I hope it's nothing serious."

"She should be released tomorrow."

"Were you picking her up? Is that what you were using for an excuse to get out of the X-rays? Because I can pick her up for you if you need me to."

I shake my head. *Quit being so nice. You're breaking my heart all over again.*

"No, thanks. Skye can manage if I can't."

"Well, let's get going, then." He stands, takes the ice pack off my foot and helps me up off the couch. I put too much pressure on my hurt foot and fall into him. He wraps his arms around me to steady me. Despite the pain in my foot, it feels good to be in his arms.

He doesn't step back or pull away, just stands there letting me rest my head on his chest, his chin resting against the top of my head.

"Did you do that on purpose?" he murmurs.

"Yeah, I twisted my ankle just so I could end up in your arms."

He makes a satisfied noise that scares me, or maybe what scares me is that I remember how safe I felt in his arms. And I like it.

When we pull apart, Tammy is standing there looking at us.

"Excuse me." She has a certain look in her eye. "What should I fix Jordan for dinner while you're gone?"

Nick looks like he's snapping back from a daze. "Oh, right, he needs to eat. Summer, sorry, love, would you mind sitting down for two minutes while I show Tammy what to fix Jordan? I'll be right back."

As he settles me on the couch, Tammy throws a last glance in our direction, and I get the distinct impression she's not comfortable with my presence.

She has all the signs of a girl in love and the sad part is, it seems Nick doesn't have a clue.

Thank God.

After he disappears into the other room, Jordan comes into the living room hugging a tattered-looking brown bear.

"This is Mr. Snuggie." He holds the bear out tentatively for me to look at him.

"Oh, hello, Mr. Snuggie. I'm Summer. It's nice to meet you."

"Nice to meet you, too." Jordan supplies the bear's voice in a raspy, falsetto little-boy tone. He holds the bear up to his ear.

"Mr. Snuggie thinks you're pretty."

I can't help but smile at him. He looks like a miniature version of Nick. Obviously, he inherited his father's charm. "Thank you, Mr. Snuggie. You're a very handsome bear."

Jordan skirts the end of the sofa, Mr. Snuggie tucked under one arm, with what looks like a wadded-up blue washcloth clenched in his fist.

"My daddy says you hurt yourself and he has to take you to the hospital."

"Yes, I was clumsy and fell down."

"Here." He holds out his hand and edges closer. I see the blue cloth is twisted into the shape of a cat or some other animal with ears. "This is my boo-boo bunny. You put ice in here." He pokes his finger through a loop in the design just large enough to hold an ice cube. "It makes boo-boos feel better. I'll get you more ice."

He starts to run out of the room, but turns back and thrusts Mr. Snuggie at me. "You can take him to the hospital with you so you won't be *a-scared*, but you have to give him back after you're done. 'Kay?"

Speechless, I stare down at the bear.

Five minutes later Nick and I are on the way to the hospital. I feel a little foolish holding the stuffed animal, but it didn't seem quite right to toss him in the backseat. Especially after Nick told me what a big deal it was that Jordan bestowed such an honor on me.

"He never lets that bear out of his sight."

"I will make sure nothing happens to it." I stare down at the animal's worn face. It's missing an eye, there's a hole near its ear and the red felt tongue is barely hanging on by a thread.

"If I can find a needle and thread at the hospital,

do you think he'd mind if I did a little surgery on Mr. Snuggie? So he doesn't lose his tongue?"

"Sure, why not?"

Nick smiles over at me and all of a sudden, it's just him and me as if we've somehow been transported back in time.

I would've preferred riding on the back of his bike, but that would have required sitting too close to him. I think I've had enough invasion of personal space to last me at least another eight years. Plus, it probably wouldn't have been very good for my foot hanging down and bumping against the bike. And where would I have put Mr. Snuggie?

We used to love taking the bike out. Just Nick and me and the open road of upstate New York. Sometimes it was as if we were the only two people in the world. We were so good together when it was just the two of us. There was an energy, a synthesis—

"Are you in Dahlia Springs because of Ginny?" He glances at me.

I nod. "She was in a bad accident, Nick. It left her in a coma for a couple of days."

"I read about the accident, but I didn't realize it

was so serious. The paper said she was stable. I thought that meant she was okay."

"She gave us a scare. I mean, we didn't know what was going to happen. But she's doing better. When we left the hospital she was awake and alert. Almost like herself except for the bruises."

He nods and there's something comforting in the way the dimple in his right cheek winks at me like an old friend. "That's great," he says. "I'm glad she's doing so well."

"Yeah, it was pretty scary at first. You never know what's going to happen when someone's in a coma, and the first few days are crucial. Nick, I was afraid she was going to die before I could get here. But…she's fine now."

"It's good you came. You never know how things are going to turn out. The people we love can slip away in a New York minute."

He glances at me again, then back at the road. Something unspoken hangs in the air between us and I know I should say something about him losing his wife.

But I can't find the words.

I'm struck by the urge to reach out and touch

him. But instead, I tuck my hands between my outer thighs and the seat.

"Since your mother's okay, how much longer are you staying?"

I shrug. "My return flight leaves Monday, but Ginny's trying to talk Skye and me into taking her to get Jane."

I roll my eyes.

His eyebrows shoot up. "Jane? Wow. What's she… um…how's she doing these days?"

"It's hard to say. Skye tracked her down. She's in a homeless shelter in Missouri. That's about all we know."

He winces. "A homeless shelter, huh? That's too bad."

"She's been gone for five years, floating from place to place. She made it clear that she didn't want to be saved. Ginny's decided enough's enough. That's why she wants us to make this trip."

"You're going?"

My foot throbs worse now than it did when I first fell. I stare out the window and suppress a sigh.

"I don't know, Nick. I'll have to see how my foot checks out."

He shoots me a look. If I let myself, I could love him all over again. A voice deep inside says, *You never stopped loving him.*

"Even if your foot's broken, you can sit with it propped up in the backseat of a car the same way you can sit with it propped up at home."

"Who says I'm going to be sitting at home?"

"I can't see you working very many catwalks in a cast, baby. You might as well indulge her. Especially in light of the accident."

I know he has to be thinking of his wife, thinking that it's unfair for me to take my mother for granted when he doesn't have a second chance with— I wonder what her name was. A headache burns in my temples.

"Ginny and I have had our issues, but seeing her like that made me realize…"

I lose my words. Or maybe I lose my nerve.

"What?"

I shrug. My mouth is dry and I really want a cigarette. "We have issues, but she's tried so hard over the past few years that I realized how much it would hurt to lose her. Now she's talking about this trip. Says she has things Skye and I need to know. Only, I don't know if I want to hear what she has to say, if it will make things better or worse. I still have to sort it all out."

His jaw works. I get the sense that he wants to say something.

"What are you thinking?" I ask.

He gives a mirthless, raspy laugh and shakes his head.

"You used to be so stubborn," he says. "Too stubborn for your own good sometimes."

"What's that supposed to mean?"

He takes a minute to answer, as if he's weighing his words. I study his profile—the full mouth; the straight nose that's a little long but somehow works with the sum of the parts; the thick, dark hair with flecks of gray at the temples and just the right amount of wave; the dense lashes the same color that frame his brown eyes. The years we've been apart have been kind to him, and my heart aches watching him.

"You're learning," he says.

I'm learning? "Learning what?"

He shakes his head and smiles, and his eyes crinkle at the edges. That old familiar Nick-longing unfurls inside of me.

"Let's just say it's good to see you step outside yourself, to include others in the scope of your world."

His words sting. Anger flares. How dare he—it hits me that this is one of those moments that I could get really pissed or... I take a deep breath. Or I could let it go.

But still I elbow him.

"Ouch!" He gives me a wry smile. "What was that for?"

"For the backhanded compliment." *For the grain of truth. For leaving me and moving on so easily.*

He slants a puzzled glance at me. "It wasn't intended to be backhanded, but if that's how you choose to take it..."

"What? If the shoe fits? I can't believe you're judging me. You have no idea what's been happening in my life over the past eight years."

This time when he looks at me, his eyes are softer.

"No, I don't know what's happening in your life and I'm sorry about that."

It takes all I have not to ask him *why* he's sorry. But I won't do it. It's bad enough that my leg hurts, but I certainly don't like feeling needy and vulnerable.

"It's been a long time." He murmurs the words, almost to himself. "Eight years is a long, long time."

We approach Baylor Road. If we hang a left, the road leads right past the tiny studio at the Shenandoah Apartments where Sky and I lived with Ginny while we were growing up.

I turn my head in the opposite direction as we pass it so I don't have to see all those memories looking back at me. Instead, I look out the passenger-side window, biting back words that want to spill out. Words like *You're sorry now, but how could you just walk away from us so easily?*

I stare down at the bear in my lap and rack my brain for something else to say to fill the silence because I'm afraid if I start down that path, he'll ask me the same question—and I won't know where to begin.

He turns on the stereo. A CD starts up mid-song. Led Zeppelin's "Stairway to Heaven." Robert Plant sings about a lady who thinks all that glitters is gold and I'm transported back in time, to the days when Nick and I first moved in together in New York. When it seemed the city held so much possibility.

He just showed up at my apartment one day.

"I'm in town applying for a job at *Geographic International*. I thought I'd look you up."

"You want to crash on my couch, don't you? That's why you're here."

The image of him standing in my doorway, leaning against the doorjamb, will be forever burned in my mind. His hair was longer then. He looked so dark and dangerous that I wondered how he'd ever been attracted to Skye. She was too straight, too bookish. Too much of a good sorority girl for this bad boy.

I was never a sorority girl.

I'd been in New York about three months. I'd signed with a small modeling agency and was getting work here and there. Just enough to make me feel anything was possible.

That's what I love about New York—the breathless feeling I got when I walked outside. It was so different from Florida's flat, wide-open spaces where the horizon lay unreachable across vast miles of ocean.

In New York anything *was* possible. There, you could get anything you wanted, be anyone you wanted. Dreams lived in these grand buildings. They were like tall boxes full of wishes come true, stacked one on top of the other. All you had to do was reach high enough and take exactly what you wanted.

Of course, that was twenty-two years ago. Since then, I've learned that even if you could reach as high as the tallest building, most of the boxes full of wishes-granted were padlocked and only a handful of players held the keys.

But I didn't know that then.

Anything seemed possible.

I asked him, "Does Skye know you're here?"

"I haven't talked to Skye in a while."

"Then come in."

He did. And he stayed.

My roommates moved out. Skye didn't talk to me for nearly four years after I finally told her.

But it was electric with Nick. From the minute I opened that door and saw him standing there until all those years later when I thought he'd walked out of my life for good.

Now it's eight years later.

"What have you been doing with yourself?" he asks.

"Still modeling for Gerard's salon."

He makes an interested noise. "You've been there a long time. How long's it been now?"

...and she's buying the stairway to heaven...

"Don't ask. How 'bout you? What have you been doing with yourself?" I brace myself for mention of his wife's death.

"Until the last year, I was traveling a lot," he says. "Shooting for *Geographic International*."

"You've stopped?"

His jaw tightens. "Gave it up for full-time fatherhood. At least for now, until a job in editorial opens. It's hard to travel so much with a kid."

I feel like such a bitch because the petty part of me wants to say, *My point exactly*. That's why I didn't want kids. The price was too high.

Then I glance down at the bear in my lap and my heart tightens.

I want to ask him if it was worth it? Giving it all up for a child? Further proof I had no business being a mother. That question wouldn't even enter the mind of a woman with the mother gene.

"I guess it's hard to have the best of both worlds," I mutter.

He doesn't answer me.

Trying my best to ignore the biting pain that's now shooting all the way up my leg, I squint my eyes and I can see the man who used to love me—the wide shoulders, that profile, the stubborn set to his jaw—as if nothing's changed. And the feelings that flood back hurt worse than my physical injury.

Robert Plant's voice fills the silence, singing about a sign on the wall and how words sometimes having two meanings. I finger the stuffed animal's faded brown fleece and wonder for a fleeting moment if the biggest mistake of my life was letting Nick walk out the door without going after him, without trying to change his mind. Or giving in and giving him a child. Could he have supplied the baby with enough love to make up for what I lacked?

Nick drives on, his left elbow resting on the door frame, as if there's nothing ironic or eerie about the music or the moment. Then the song shifts into the guitar riff, shattering the illusion and I turn off the stereo.

Clumsy quiet fills the car and I can't stand it.

"I can't believe you have a son."

"He's the best thing that's ever happened to me, Summer."

His words stir a pang, and my thoughts shift again to the boy's mother. I wonder how often Nick thinks of her and if he's still hurting. Stupid question. Of course he still hurts. Even *I* hurt for him losing her and I never met the woman who got the man I loved.

What kind of life did they have? Was she pretty? Did she make him forget me?

She must have been a hell of a woman to entice the ramblin' man to give up his travels for such a bourgeois existence. But really, as it turned out, that's what he wanted, wasn't it?

And now she's dead.

I'm not good at dealing with death. I'm totally inept at condolences because I can never find the right words. I usually end up standing there like a dolt, stammering something useless and wooden like *I'm sorry*.

How is apologizing supposed to help? Seems like all it does is rip open the healing wound.

Strains of Elton John's "Sorry Seems to Be The Hardest Word" float through my head.

I feel selfish because the part of the song that resonates with me is when he asks, "What have I got to do to make you love me?"

But as I stare out the window, watching the line

of anonymous cars roll by, I remind myself this isn't about me. I have to say something. I must…

"Nick, I heard about you losing your wife. And I'm…*sorry*." The words bite, but I force myself to look him in the eyes.

I swear I see him flinch.

A slight frown pulls down his face and his throat works.

"Is there anything I can do for you and Jordan?"

He looks at me with rueful eyes. My heart aches for him. And Jordan, too, I suppose.

"Maybe there is," he says. "But right now I don't know what."

CHAPTER 8

Skye

In the dream, I'm eleven years old and I'm lying next to Summer on the foldout couch in the living room of our old studio apartment off Baylor Road.

The dream starts off the same way it always has since the first time I dreamed it who knows how many years ago. Oh Lord, as far back as I can remember.

Anyway, it starts with Summer asleep, but I'm wide awake, anxious because it's midnight and Mama's not home yet.

My stomach feels swollen with worry and I wish I could just go to sleep like Summer.

The Big Ben travel alarm we use for a clock sits on the end table giving off a greenish phosphorescent glow. Thin slips of light filter through the vertical blinds that don't hang right on the sliding glass doors. The long, pale yellow strands remind me of the spaghetti noodles I cooked for dinner for Summer and me since Mama was out.

She's been out a long time tonight.

I turn on my side and count the flowers on the wallpaper: one hundred and two from floor to ceiling; fifty-nine from the corner to where the wallpaper disappears behind the big painting of the beach that was hanging on the wall when we moved in. I count again, sure that Mama will be home before I finish.

But she's not.

So I flop over on my back and pick out pictures in the popcorn ceiling. The dim light always gives them more dimension, more contrast than if you look for them in the daylight. I can see a dog and an angel and a palm tree. I keep looking because tonight I'm sure I won't see the monster in the ceiling.

I'm not afraid.

Really, I'm not.

But when the door opens and I hear Mama's voice and a man's voice, the monster in the ceiling pops out, snarling at me with bulging eyeballs and big, ugly fangs. I have to squeeze my eyes shut tight to make sure the fiend doesn't break free and eat us all up.

But just closing my eyes isn't enough. I know that. I have to keep them shut for a slow count of three hundred thirty-three—no more, no less—to make sure the monster goes away. I don't know why three hundred thirty-three is the magic number.

It just is.

Eighteen…nineteen…twenty…

Even though I hear Mama and I want to tell her I'm so glad she's home because I was worried she wouldn't come back tonight, I don't dare open my eyes.

Because if I open them too soon, even though the monster might seem like it's gone, it'll still be there, hiding somewhere in the apartment and come back to get us after Mama's gone to sleep on her pallet over in the corner behind the dressing screen that she put up for *privacy*.

Twenty-eight…twenty-nine…thirty…

She laughs her dainty little laugh and the man talks. Not the same man who was here last night. I can tell on account of his different voice. He smells the same as all the others, though, a pungent odor of that strong stuff Mama drinks and cigarette smoke and like he needs to take a bath.

She shushes him like she does all the others she

brings home and mumbles, "You've got to keep quiet if I let you in here. My babies are asleep on the couch. Don't you dare wake them up."

Thirty-eight…thirty-nine…forty…

I hear sucking and smacking noises. The man is mouth breathing, real heavy, like he can't get enough air and is drinking in great, greedy gulps. Mama giggles and whispers, "No, not here. Let's go over there, but you've gotta be gone before sunup."

Forty-eight…forty-nine…fifty…

Their feet shuffle on the shag carpet and the man rams into the foot of our bed with such force I think the couch is going to turn over. Without even opening my eyes, I know he was the one who hit the bed because he says, "Shit," and a string of other bad words.

Mama shushes him again.

Fifty-eight…fifty-nine…sixty.

Then there's something that sounds like zippers unzipping and quiet moans and muffled cries and I worry that the monster's gotten Mama with all those noises she's making. It sounds like something real bad's happening to her over there in the corner.

Should I go help her even though I'm not done

counting? Last night she was okay after she made those noises. And she was okay all the times before that.

"Mama?" I whisper.

She doesn't answer, just moans some more. I plug my ears and keep counting.

One hundred one…one hundred two…one hundred three…

Sure enough, by the time I reach three hundred thirty-three, the apartment is quiet again, except for the sound of the man's snores.

I open my eyes, blink a few times in the darkness to get my vision back. The monster in the ceiling is gone. I get out of my bed and creep silent as a kitten over to make sure my mama's still alive.

She's lying there naked, one arm thrown back over her head.

I'm so afraid I shake. It's that sick kind of scared that spreads slowly through your body, freezing you from the inside out.

The man's naked, too. And that makes me feel even worse. He's lying spread-eagle on his back. I won't let myself have a good look at him. I don't want to see him and his *thing* all slimy and disgusting like a shriveled caterpillar sleeping in a hairy nest at the base of his big, fat belly.

Patty Spivey told me that sometimes men put their *things* inside women. But I didn't believe her.

She's never even seen a man's *thing*.

I wonder what she'd do if she knew I had?

I realize my eyes have wandered over his body while I was thinking about Patty. I feel so strange and dirty like I know I shouldn't be looking at him. I don't want to and I *don't* want to think of this ugly, hairy beast putting anything inside my beautiful Mama.

I force my eyes away and train my eyes real hard on Mama's flat, porcelain stomach until I see it move up and down in a steady one-two rhythm.

Breathe in.

Breathe out.

I want to puke, and once I know that she's alive, I crawl back in my bed, next to Summer, who's slept through the whole thing, and keep my eyes closed so I don't look up at the ceiling.

Then the dream changes, like dreams will do. I'm floating above the scene—it's no longer our apartment, it's a nondescript room, but the man is still there and when I see the face of the girl he's covering with his massive body, it's Jane. Her vacant brown eyes look almost hollow.

She looks…dead.

Jane, no! Oh, Jane, please no—

My own keening wakes me up. Disoriented, I push into a sitting position from the ball I'd curled into. I'm shaking and sweating and vaguely nauseated. It takes a few seconds before I realize I'm in Mama's living room on the couch.

I fell asleep.

It was just a dream.

Thank God. Tears threaten to flow and I wonder if I can make them stop.

Oh my God, Jane. Jane, are you okay?

My heart beats so loudly it seems to echo throughout the entire quiet house. I never knew a place could be as still as it is now and I bury my face in my hands to try to blot out the image of Jane's dead eyes.

Oh, dear God, make it stop.

The raspberry cobbler I ate bubbles up in the back of my throat.

"It was just a dream." I say the words aloud to convince myself. To block out the warring voice inside me that asks, *Or was it?*

I hug my knees to me. The dream scares me on so many levels: First, because I know that life on the street is dangerous and Jane is at risk every day she's out there alone without a roof over her head.

But I'm not a believer in precognitive dreams.

So what does it mean? That I'm worried about my sister? That we've let her drift long enough?

It's bad enough that the memories of Mama's indiscretions still plague me after all the years.

It's disturbing, embarrassing. It makes me feel dirty.

In college, I had a basic psychology class and in it, I did a report on Freud's theory that dreams are the pathway to encounters buried in the subconscious. That in childhood everyone has forbidden sexual desire, things so frightening they can't face them in conscious thought. He claimed these hidden desires manifested in dreams as strange creatures and frightening events.

Yuck.

My own sex life is stale, but I dream of my mother and her boyfriends? That's wrong.

What Mama did was inappropriate, bringing all those men in and having sex with them while Summer and I were right there in the room.

Mama was usually drunk and I suppose she thought we were asleep. I'm sure it never occurred to her that one of them might harm us…maybe that's what the part about Jane was all about.

I don't know.

I rarely dream in such vivid detail. In fact, just about the only time I remember my dreams is when I have the one about the monster in the ceiling. Usually, it ends with me lying down next to Summer. And I wake up. It always leaves me with the same disgusted feeling.

Until I push it aside and do the exercise my therapist taught me: In my head I visualize a perfect childhood. Exorcise the ceiling monster with a dream in which my sisters, mother and I are at peace with one another. Where everything is normal and safe. Where there are hugs and home-baked cookies, a sandbox in the backyard, a grandmother who loved us….

The images are fleeting.

In my head, I can make the cookies appear. I can make them disappear.

The monster is there. Then he's not.

The monster is there, but he walks away from Jane without killing her.

Horrific images try to elbow their way from my mind's shadows, but there's not enough light for them to break through.

It's all a dream. It's not real—the dream of the ceiling monster is *not* real; the dream of Jane with dead eyes is *not* real.

I hug my knees and rock back and forth.

All that matters is the here and now, that we're going to see Jane in a few days.

CHAPTER 9

Summer

Nick drops me off at Ginny's house after midnight. My damn foot's broken. It's bundled in a huge bootlike contraption and the doctor says it'll be at least six weeks of staying off my feet before I'm healed. I have no idea what I'm going to tell Gerard. He can't very well fit clothing on me while I'm sitting down.

Nick walks me to the door, and we stand on the porch like teenagers on a first date. Maneuvering the crutches and the bag of pills from the twenty-four-hour pharmacy, I reach for the knob, a little unsteady on my feet. Nick is faster than I am and opens the door for me. Thank God, Skye left it unlocked so I didn't have to ring the bell and wait for her to let me in. This is awkward enough without factoring her into the mix.

I step inside, stopping on the threshold, taking my

time turning and hoping Nick will get the hint that I don't want him to come in. I'm too tired, too woozy from the pain medicine and, despite the drugs, my foot throbs through the numbed fog.

Still, he touches my elbow. "Let me help you inside."

I pull away, stumble a little.

He grabs my arm and steadies me. And it's sick because the feel of his hand on my arm gives me a rush.

"You broke your foot. Let me help you."

"No, really, it's best if you don't."

"I just want to help you in and make sure you don't fall and break something else."

I jab a finger at his chest. "Just go away. I can manage fine without you."

There's an uncomfortable silence and the words hang in the air, like a punching bag inviting him to a verbal sparring match. I can't look at him, so I stare over his left shoulder, blinking away the occasional double image when my eyes won't focus.

We hold the standoff for what seems an eternity. Until finally I say, "Skye's here."

He gives me a *so what* shrug.

"Just go home unless you want Tammy to spend the night."

Although, I'm sure that's exactly what Tammy would love to do. But you really should go home to your little boy.

"Fine." I watch him walk away, then hesitate and glance back at me. Under the amber porch light he looks like he's still eighteen years old. But then his image shifts out of focus. I blink and he looks just like he did when he left me.

"I'll call you later to see what you've decided to do about this trip with Ginny. Maybe you should consider it since you can't go back to work for a while. It might do you some good to hear her out."

His words wedge themselves into the cracks in my armor. My defenses want to ask him why. Why call now? After all these years? But instead, I nod and hobble inside so I won't have to watch him disappear into the darkness.

I shut myself inside the cool, dim foyer and stand light-headed and at war with myself, my back pressed against the door. I close my eyes trying to steady myself. For a moment, I can almost feel him fading back into my life.

But then I open my eyes and glance around at the strange surroundings. Nothing's familiar and I wonder if eventually I'll awaken in my bed in my apartment in New York to find out this whole trip has been a bizarre dream.

Voices emanate from the other room. Skye must be watching television. I hobble in and see her dozing on the couch, her head on a small velvet pillow, a blue velour blanket over her legs. The remote control is still in her hand.

As I move toward the television to turn it off, the rubber tip of my crutches squeaks on the marble floor and the sound awakens her. She yawns and squints at me.

"Oh my goodness, look at you." She stretches and pushes herself into a sitting position. "Is it broken?"

I nod. "Snapped like a twig."

Skye hops up off the couch and tries to help me. I shake her off. "Thank you, but I'm not an invalid."

She frowns. "Who said you were?" She turns off the television, then takes my crutches and lays them across the coffee table as I settle myself into the corner of the sofa and hoist my boot-covered leg onto the cushions. The effort makes my head swim in a drug-induced fog. It's hard to focus on her, because she's moving around, gathering up pillows, shoving them under my foot. My head lolls back into the cushion.

"What is it with everyone fussin' over me? I'm fixin' to live like this for a while so I'm a gonna have to learn to manage by myself."

Skye laughs.

I blink at her. Why is she laughing at me? I am in no mood.

"What the hell is so funny?"

She shakes her head and smirks. "They must have you on some powerful good drugs because your Southern accent is slippin' through, sister dear."

My mouth is numb, but I still feel my upper lip curl. "Don't be absurd." I can't be sure, but I think I just slurred my words. Why can't this medicine numb my pain the way it's numbed me everywhere else?

She just keeps going on and on and on. Her eyes are watering she's laughing so hard and it sets something inside *a me* to boil...er...I mean, it pisses me off. It *really* pisses me off.

"You've taken such pains to get rid of your accent," she says. "To be so citified, and in the span of two sentence you said *fussin'*, *fixin'* and *gonna*. Say it again—"

"Shut up, Skye. Just *shut* up."

She stands there with her mouth open, forming a small "oh." Instantly, I regret saying it. "I'm sorry—"

She shakes her head and turns her back on me. I can't see her face from my place on the couch.

Oh my God, is she crying?

Skye is prone to bouts of martyrdom and fits of rage. She can be as cold as a winter day. But tears have never been her style. In fact, I can't recall ever having seen her cry.

One time when we were kids, maybe eleven or twelve, Ginny was in a mood and, of course, I was pushing her buttons. I wanted to go to a party at a friend's house, but she didn't want to drive me.

So I decided I'd walk the three miles and left without telling her because I was mad at her for not taking me. I'd gotten about a mile down the road when Ginny drove up behind me in her old beat-up green Buick.

It was dusk and there were no streetlights on the highway back then. So when she stopped the car, I walked back to meet her because I thought she'd come to drive me the rest of the way. Instead, she dragged me by my hair into the car and didn't say a word to me until we got home. Then all she said was, "Get out." She had the devil in her eyes, and I knew I'd better do what she said.

Once we were inside the apartment, she went into her bedroom and got the belt she used on us when we misbehaved.

Well, just seeing her come out of the room with that thing made me scream. I started bawling before she'd even hit me, begging her not to. But she did and the harder I cried the harder she hit me, until the next thing I knew, Skye grabbed the belt from Ginny's hand and tossed it out of her reach.

Then Ginny started beating on Skye with her bare hands, and Skye just stood there like a stone statue taking it until Ginny finally wore herself out.

She never shed one tear and, thinking back, I can't remember seeing her cry—ever. Not when Ginny beat us or left us or went days without saying a word to us. Skye was the mother hen, the protector taking care of us all when Ginny checked out.

"Skye, really, I'm sorry. That was uncalled-for. You didn't deserve that."

"No, I didn't." She turns toward me and her face

is set like stone. Not a trace of moisture in her eyes. "I deserve to be treated a lot better."

She walks out of the room. If my mind was swimming because of the painkillers, this confrontation shifts it into a downward spiral that pins me to the couch.

I sit alone, listening to the sound of her footsteps retreat up the staircase, until silence hums in my ears. I run my hand along the cracked surface of the leather couch.

It takes me more than five minutes to navigate the stairs, but somehow, I manage to maneuver the crutches up the steps without falling and breaking another bone.

The hall light is on, illuminating the long expanse of marble covered by an expensive, narrow Oriental rug that stretches the length of the corridor.

I train my ear to see if I can detect any sounds, but only the quiet answers me.

The longer I stand there wondering where to begin, the more I feel the grouping of photos in the hallway is mocking me.

I am not the comforter, not the one who's kept us all together despite all that's happened. That's been

Skye's doing. If it were left to me it probably would've all gone out the window because, despite outward appearances, I'm not the strong one. Fearing that Skye will fall apart dredges up all the unhappiness we've harbored over the years.

I've heard of people finding themselves in their unhappiness, but I've never understood this concept. I've been searching for nearly twenty-five years, (I suppose Ginny's been looking even longer than that), and I have yet to find answers.

I always thought Skye had it together. But, I don't know, it seems like we're back at the starting line, queuing up as we have in the past, only to leave more fractured than when we started. All because we're trying to pretend we're a happy, normal family.

Why are we doing this?

Because we're stuck in some sick cycle that we can't break free of? I wonder what it is that's so pressing that Ginny has to tell us and that propels me forward.

I hobble over to the room next to mine—choosing it because it's the only one with a closed door—and knock softly. "Skye?"

She doesn't answer.

I twist the knob and push the door open. She's sitting on her bed. Her face is expressionless.

Her room is done in various shades of blue—blue carpet, blue walls, blue comforter and pillows. The blue room, I think as Skye looks at me with unreadable eyes.

"You shouldn't be climbing stairs on those crutches."

"You didn't leave me much of a choice, did you, running up here like that?"

She shrugs. "Sorry."

The crutches are digging in under my arms, and I shift to get more comfortable. To no avail. They've already rubbed me raw. I wonder if it's possible for one to develop armpit calluses?

"Here, Summer, you shouldn't be on your feet. Sit down." She pats the mattress and picks up a pillow and hugs it to her middle.

Resting her chin on the top of the pillow, she eyes me as I make my way to the side of the bed. I brace myself for one of her lectures.

"Isn't it funny the way things turn out?" she says. "Here we are forty years old in Mama's big house, in the fancy bedrooms we never had." She runs her hand over the silk duvet cover. "You know if I could have decorated a room when we were growing up, it would have been just like this."

"Blue? I always had you pegged for more of a pink person."

She shrugs. "Cameron wants me to come home."

"When?"

The air conditioner cycles on and a rush of cold air washes over me.

"Right now, if he had his way. Tomorrow, or as soon as we get Mama settled."

"Are you leaving?"

Her shoulders rise and fall.

"I don't know what I'm going to do." She squeezes the bridge of her nose.

I reach out and touch her back. "What's the matter? This isn't like you."

"I'm a mess." She swipes at her nose. "A complete and utter mess."

Shaking my head, I say, "If you're a mess, what does that make me? You're more together than most people I know."

I squeeze her arm and smile. She makes a lame attempt to push up the corners of her mouth, and says, "Do you remember how Mama used to bring men home when we were little?"

She pulls away from me and crosses her arms over her chest.

"Well, yeah, there were so many of them."

"Do you ever remember anything…happening?"

"What do you mean?"

Shadows of prickly memories swim to the surface and I fight to push them down.

"Nothing. Never mind." She stands up suddenly, walks into the bathroom, turns on the faucet. I sit on the bed holding my breath, trying to think of anything but the sad lineup of men Ginny used to bring home. The only thing they had in common is that they usually were drunk and they never stayed. Around the time we were turning eleven, Ginny stopped dating. Of course I didn't know that at the time, but all the pieces fit now. I wonder why Sky brought it up?

A minute later, she comes back into the bedroom, drying her face on a fluffy, light-blue hand towel.

"Summer, I'm sorry to act like this. It's just that Cameron's mad that I'm here…." She trails off, wringing the towel.

"Go home if your family needs you."

She waves me off. "The kids couldn't care less. They don't need me. They need a maid. And a chauffeur. Any able body with a driver's license and a vague idea of how to boil water will do."

The medication is making me woozy. I see two of her and I blink.

"Okay, so don't go home. Let them find another able body. I'm sure the person won't do things quite the way you do. If you're gone maybe they'll miss you."

Oh, it's so easy to play armchair quarterback. I'm half expecting my sister to remind me of that.

"But what if they don't? What if life goes on just as well without me? My kids are growing up, Summer. Pretty soon they'll be out on their own and, well, basically I'll be out of a job."

I want to say, *That's a good thing. You'll have more time for you. You'll get to do the things you want to do.* But it hits me that me-time is probably a foreign concept to my sister. This is one of those times when the fundamental differences in our personalities glare so brightly I can barely see past it. But then I hear myself saying, "By coming here, Skye, I've put my identity on the line, too."

"Your *identity?* Isn't that a little dramatic?"

"No it's not. I'm terrified that while I'm gone, Gerard will discover he can get along just fine without me in the studio. That I'll go back to New York to learn I'm out of a job." I rap my knuckles on the boot. "Now that I've got this to contend with, I don't have a choice but to sit out a while and see what happens. Do I?"

She straightens a little, seems more like herself. "You'll be fine."

"And so will you. In fact, it might be good for us to step outside ourselves for a while."

Nick's words: *Step outside of yourself. Include others in the scope of your world.*

She doesn't say anything, only looks at me as if I've presented a complicated mathematical theory and she's mentally checking my work.

"I'll make a deal with you," I say. "If you go on this trip with Ginny, I'll arrange a leave of absence from the studio and go, too. With this foot, I won't be able to work anyway."

I guess in our own different ways, it's no more of a burden than Skye having to tell her husband and arranging for someone to look in on her three kids.

Is it convenient?

No.

Is it something we'd choose to do?

Hell no.

Despite it all, we know we have to go.

When Ginny had the accident it was as if something that had been simmering in the murky part of our lives that we don't talk about shifted and rushed to the surface.

"Will you do it?" I ask her.

CHAPTER 10

Skye

We bring Mama home from the hospital shortly after one o'clock. Dr. Travis gave her the all-clear, which she took as carte blanche for this crazy wild-goose chase she wants to drag us on, and that's all she talked about from that moment on.

She was about to drive me crazy. To preserve our sanity, Summer and I got her settled in and went to "run a few errands." I hated to go off and leave Mama so soon after her homecoming, but her prattle was about to drive me right up the foil-papered walls.

In the car, the silence is like balm to my ears. I don't even turn on the radio as I head south on Organza Street toward downtown.

When we walk into Joe's Fountain, the diner connected to the drugstore, the bell over the door sounds.

"Be right with you," sings Jodie Marsh from the kitchen. "Grab a seat anywhere ya want."

We chose a table in the corner because it'll afford us more privacy. Not that privacy is at a premium given that aside from Jodie we're the only ones in the fountain this afternoon. But in Dahlia Springs, even seemingly empty rooms have been know to sprout ears, so it's best to take care.

Summer looks around. "My God, this place looks exactly the same. Remember how we used to love to come to work with Ginny and sit up there at the bar?" She grabs a menu. "Do they still make fresh-squeezed limeade?"

A Muzak version of "Flowers on The Wall" plays through the overhead speakers.

Jodie, who's managed the fountain for as far back as I can remember—even when Mama worked here—starts over to take our order.

A heavyset blonde with coffee-colored eyes and a contagious laugh as thick and rich as maple syrup, Jodie saved Mama's hide (and her job) more than once back in the day when things weren't so good. Being a small town, word *got around* that Ginny Galloway got around and it brought a little bit of trouble into the fountain until Mama cleaned herself up and flew right. But Jodie was always right there with her.

As Jodie approaches our table, an ear-piercing scream breaks free and she throws her arms around Summer's neck. "Summer Galloway, as I live and breathe. I heard you was back in town."

"And Skye Woods, I'll declare. Honey, I was beginning to wonder when you were going to come in and see me."

She covers her mouth with a pudgy hand and shakes her head. "Wonderful news about your mama. I heard Ginny's gone home from the hospital."

This might be a new record. Mama's been home just over two hours and the whole town knows.

"Jodie, it's good to see you," says Summer. "You haven't changed a bit."

"Oh, I've gotten so fat." She pats her round belly and shrugs. "Hazard of the job. Someone's gotta test the pies to make sure they're fit to eat." She throws her head back and unleashes a guffaw that teases a smile to our lips.

She reaches out and tweaks my upper arm. "I see someone else has been testing some pie, missy."

More laughter. On her part. That wasn't funny.

"So what'll y'all have, girls?" She whips her order pad from her apron pocket and pulls a pen from behind her ear. "I got some peach pie that'll curl your toes." *Ha-ha-ha*. "Skye, we gotta get some meat on your sister's bones. A strong breeze'll come blowin' down Main Street and sweep her on out to sea if we don't."

I smile, wishing something would carry Jodie off so Summer and I can discuss what we came to talk about.

"No, thank you. No pie for me," I say. "Just iced tea, unsweetened with lemon."

"And black coffee for me, Jodie." Summer smiles at her warmly.

The large woman frowns, puts a hand on her hip. "Oh, come on, you girls are on vacation. Throw caution to the wind." She sweeps her arms out wide. "At least make it sweet tea."

Vacation? Right.

"No, thank you." I conjure my most polite voice. "That'll do us."

The way Jodie shrugs and shoves her pen back behind her ear, it almost seems she's taken our liquid order as a personal insult.

Two minutes later she sets our beverages in front

of us. "Well, if you change your mind. I'll be back in the kitchen."

We watch her saunter back to the snack bar and disappear into the kitchen.

Summer says, "What are you going to do about this trip?"

I take a long sip of tea. *Mmm, it's good.*

"Did you stop to think about whether you really want to know what Mama has to tell us?" I ask. "I mean, we've gone all these years without knowing…."

Summer blows her coffee and takes a testing sip.

"So it's not really Cameron you're afraid of, it's Ginny's deep dark secrets?"

"I'm not *afraid* of either." Oh, how to put this. "Summer, it's that dream. Where we're back in the old apartment at the Shenandoah. The problem is, the other night there was more to the dream. It was Jane. I dreamed she was dead."

Summer winces.

"All along, I've had trepidations about this trip, because I'm not sure Jane wants to be found. She's twenty-one years old and if she wanted to come home, she would."

Summer sips her coffee. "*We* don't even like coming home."

The bell on the door jingles. Jodie yells her greeting from the back, and old Jed Farley saunters up to the snack bar. He does a double take at Summer and me. Nods and takes a seat on one of the stools. Thanks goodness, he's a man of few words.

"Are you sure you don't want to split a piece of the peach pie?" I ask Summer.

"*Oh*, why not?"

After Jodie takes Jed's order, we signal her over. "Okay, you win. We'll live dangerously and split a piece of the peach pie you tempted us with."

Jodie beams and floats off to serve us up some of her prized confection.

She puts a scoop of vanilla ice cream in a dish on the side. "I forgot to ask ya if you wanted it à la mode, but the way y'alls had your heads together, I can tell you're talking about something important, so I just put it on the side."

The subtext of Jodie's observation was: I'm all ears if you'd care to share. I'll turn up my hearing aid if you don't.

I spoon a little dollop of ice cream onto my side

of the warm pie. It melts as I break through the flaky crust with my fork and claim my first bite.

Summer watches me as I chew. "So are we going on this trip or not?"

My gaze skips from Jed's broad back clad in his old blue work shirt to attentive Jodie smiling from behind the snack bar.

"Another piece, hon?"

"No, Jodie, but this is delicious."

If I'd had a bit of hesitation earlier about going to find my little sister, it's all gone now.

Summer

When Skye and I get home, Ginny is sitting at the kitchen table drinking a cup of tea and looking at a magazine. The room smells of her Opium perfume. It's a little heavy for a hot August day. Or maybe it's affecting me that way because I'm dizzy from the pain medication and the talk I just had with my sister.

Our mother's changed clothes. She's donned a hot-pink-and-blue floral blouse. She looks electric in the bright colors with her blond, blond hair flipping up at the shoulders, bubblegum-pink lips and swipes of matching blush racing across her cheekbones.

She's ba-ack.

I want to take a tissue and tone her down a decibel or two.

But that's Ginny. Love her or leave her.

"Do you have any maps?" I ask.

She blinks. "Maps…?" Her head tilts to the right and she squints at us, as if she wants to hear us say the actual words before she'll let herself believe it.

"So we can map out a route to get Jane," I say. "Unless you've changed your mind."

She claps her hands. "Lord have mercy, no, I haven't changed my mind. So you'll go? Really?"

I nod.

She covers her heart with her right hand.

"Oh, my soul!" Jumping up, she hugs us one at a time. It's hard to believe that less than forty-eight hours ago she was in the hospital. She feels small and fragile. I don't want to squeeze her too tightly because I'm afraid she'll break.

When she pulls away, she's positively beaming and beautiful despite the deep purple ringing her left eye. I'm glad we decided to do this.

It feels right, in a strange, off-kilter sort of way.

"Land's sakes, I have about a million things to do before we leave. I have some foundation appointments I'll have to get Raul to reschedule. I have to pack and get my hair done and I need to go over to the drugstore and get some heavy-duty concealer for this eye." She presses her fingertips to her cheekbone. "I must look a frightful sight. Oh, and I'd better get to the bank."

Skye frowns. "That's a lot to do, Mama. Are you sure you're up to this? Maybe we should wait?"

"Absolutely not. Carpe diem, babies. Carpe diem."

Skye's hand flutters to the scoop neck of her blouse. I notice a patchwork of red splotches across her décolletage. I wonder if she's having second thoughts. I hope not, because I already called Gerard and told him about my accident, that I was taking a few extra days off (for the trip, but he didn't need the details, I'm sure he didn't have time to hear them) and I might need some time off my feet. Less than thrilled, he said he'd see what he could figure out, but he had deadlines. Designs couldn't come to a halt waiting for me to heal.

So nice to feel loved and needed.

Still, I've always wanted to try my hand at designing, but it's never seemed like the right time. Until now. I tossed out the suggestion of assisting with the designs. He said he'd think about it.

"We have to make this trip quick." Skye's words are clipped. "Cameron's going to have a fit. We can't linger."

Ginny puts her hands on her slim hips. "Of course, darlin'. I wasn't expectin' to linger. Not in Springvale. If I was going to linger anywhere with you girls, I'd take you somewhere spectacular. And you know what? Someday we'll do that. Where would you like to go?"

"First things first, Ginny. Let's get through this trip and then we'll talk about the next one, okay?"

"I'll hold you to that. I better go upstairs and get to work. I have so much to do."

"Mama, I have a question for you, before you go."

"Sure, sweetie, what is it?"

"You were born in Springvale. How is it that Jane's ended up there?"

"Don't you remember, I took Jane to see my mother before she died? Jane was six years old."

Skye arches a brow. Ginny must read something

in the expression, because right away she gets defensive. "Now you remember, I called and asked you girls to come."

Skye shakes her head. "No, I don't remember."

"Sure," I said. "Ginny tried to get us to go with her, but we couldn't. I don't know what you were doing, but I had to work. I couldn't take time off."

Ginny looks off into the distance as if she's trying to remember.

"I hadn't spoken to Mother since...well, we hadn't spoken in a long time. A cousin of mine who lived in Springvale called me and told me that Mother had had a heart attack. I took Jane to meet her. I thought taking Jane to her was the decent thing to do. We only spent three days with her, but we made amends. And I'm glad. Because she died two months later. I suspect Jane went there looking for the love her grandmother showed her. Because she never would let me love her. She took to Jane just like she loved you girls—" Ginny stops midsentence, her mouth forming an O.

"What do you mean *just like she loved us?*" I ask. "We never met Grandma Ina."

Ginny glances back and forth between the two of

us, looking a little nervous. She obviously slipped, because we never knew we met Grandma Ina. Ginny always maintained that it was because of a long-standing feud that had separated them.

"When?" Skye demands.

"I'll make a deal with you. I'll tell you all about it once we're on the road. Okay? I have a lot to do."

As she walks out of the kitchen I hear her say, "Maps! I'll call my travel agent and get her to plan us out a route."

Her aura lingers even after she clears the room. The silence is deafening. Skye stands with her back against the wall, one arm crossed over her middle, chewing the cuticle on the other hand.

Skye shakes her head. "Why do I get the feeling we're in for a wild ride?"

I smile at her. "So you haven't told Cameron. I thought you were going to call him this morning?"

She studies her fingernails. "Later today, maybe, but not right now."

"Skye, are you okay?"

She looks me straight in the eye. "I'm fine. I don't want to talk about it." It's very clear that she means business.

She frowns and shrugs. "I don't think this is a good idea, and frankly, I can't believe I ever agreed to do it."

I hear Nick's voice in my head. "It's good you're thinking outside of yourself." A rush of feelings I can't quite identify courses through me and I shove them back into the shadows. It shouldn't matter what he thinks.

Oh, but it does.

Skye draws in a deep breath but doesn't say anything.

"Look, you're not backing out now. We've already told her we'd go. Besides, I can't drive with my foot in this thing. If I leave all the driving to Ginny she's liable to kill us both. If you'll remember, her less-than-stellar driving is why we're here in the first place."

My joke doesn't make her smile. So I walk over to the wall and pick up the phone. "What's Cameron's office number?"

"What? Summer!"

"What's his office number? Or would it be better to call his cell phone?"

"Hang up, Summer. I told you I'm not ready to talk to him now."

"I know you're not. That's why I'm doing it for you. If you don't tell me, I'll call Information. His number?"

She huffs a little exasperated sound.

"He's in court right now. You won't reach him."

"All the better. I'll just leave him a message. Or you can."

She opens her mouth as if she's going to object, then grabs the phone. "Fine."

She punches in a number.

A moment later she says, "His voice mail," and looks relieved.

Before she speaks, it's so quiet I can hear the refrigerator hum.

"Cameron, hi. It's me." She turns her back while she talks. "Look, I've decided to go on this trip with Mama and Summer—because it's...it's important. *Um*, you and the kids will be fine without me for a week or so. And Becky can help with Sydney and Cole. It'll be good for her to have some responsibility. Call me when you get a chance. We're leaving tomorrow morning, early. Thank you for understanding, sweetheart. I love you."

She hangs up and turns to me wide-eyed.

"There," I say. "That wasn't so bad, was it?"

She blows out an audible breath, closes her eyes for a moment. "Well, I'm glad it's over. I wonder how long it's going to take him to call back and start screaming? I'll probably never hear the end of it."

"Then don't answer your phone."

She does a double take, as if the concept never occurred to her. "I don't think so. I don't run away from things, Summer. I make it my rule to face situations head-on."

My eyebrows knit. "Right, such as how you jumped right in there and called Cameron. I see."

She looks at me. "I called him. And I would have done so without your prodding. I just wasn't ready right then."

"And you did just fine not being ready."

"You are such a bully. Always have been." She ends up opting for disgust, shaking her head and walking over to the stove.

"Actually, *you've* always been the bossy one. But thank you. It was fun stepping out of my role for a change."

"You're welcome. Do you want some tea?"

"Sure, why not."

She measures the water and puts the kettle on to boil. As she takes two china mugs from the cupboard, my purse starts ringing.

"Hello?"

"How's the foot?"

When I hear Nick's voice, my stomach spirals all the way to my toes. He's calling just as he promised.

"It hurts, but I have no time to think about that because I'm taking a road trip with my mother. And my sister. To get my other sister."

"I'm glad you're going. Any chance I can see you before you leave?"

Later that night Nick and Jordan take me to the Dairy Queen to get ice cream. I'd be lying if I said I wasn't a little disappointed that the date was a threesome.

Jordan's a great kid, but therein lies the flaw.

He's a kid.

His presence reminds me of why Nick and I are no longer Nick and I. Contrary to what he seems to want to believe, I have not grown a *mother gene* since the last time we saw each other.

It makes me feel a tad claustrophobic. This is

what *families* do. Anyone who didn't know us would think we were a *family*—that I was Jordan's—oh God, I can't even say it.

People who *do* know us will think that we're considering becoming a *family*.

But I don't want to step into the role of mother. Like a replacement part for a broken household appliance.

Women like Tammy are made for that role.

Sitting at the Dairy Queen picnic table, I try to superimpose a mental picture of Tammy as the mother in their happy little threesome.

But that doesn't work, either.

I get a little jealous pang.

A feeling, even more unpalatable, seeps in as we're in the car on the way home. Jordan's in the backseat singing a kid song to himself and I'm sure it's adorable. If I could find something like that adorable. I'm sitting next to Nick in the car and he takes my hand, lacing his fingers through mine. The warmth of his skin on mine takes my breath away.

I try to see Tammy sitting next to him. Nick holding her hand.

Uh-uh. Can't see it.

The worst one is after I say good-night to Jordan

and he's safely tucked away inside the car. Nick tells him to stay put while he walks me to the door.

"I'll just be one minute."

He steps inside, and for a few glorious seconds it's just Nick and me and he kisses me, soft and deep like he used to.

And there's no way I will even try to picture him doing that to Tammy. Especially when he whispers, "God, it's good to see you," and his lips are a breath away from mine.

Oh, God, I'm slipping.

CHAPTER 11

Ginny

We're on the highway somewhere in the Florida Panhandle. It's so nice, this on-the-road togetherness. Just me with both of my girls—Skye's driving us in her fancy car, and my beautiful Summer is in the backseat with that broken foot of hers. I nearly swell with pride from it.

And the cherry on top is knowing that by this time tomorrow, I'll see my Jane.

I wonder how she's going to act when she sees us standing there? I wonder how I'll act, what I'll say.

It's been so long. Too long. I know now that I shouldn't have let it go on this long, but I didn't always see it that way. It made more sense to let her be. I was afraid that if I made too rash a move that she'd disappear completely. Maybe that sounds like a lame excuse, but it made sense at the time.

I know I wasn't a good mother, but I can't help but feel I must have done *something* right since my twins are here with me, willing to haul me all the way to Missouri and back. It was a stretch that they both came down here to be with me—Summer especially coming all the way from New York. Don't you know I was surprised when I opened my eyes and saw them standing next to my bed? I thought it was a dream, I truly did.

Part of me just wants to ask them *why* they're here. I don't want them to take it the wrong way. I'm glad they're here. It's silly, I know, asking them *why?* Okay, I'll admit it. I want to hear them say, *We're here because we love you, Mama. Because you're our mother and this is what daughters do.*

No, Virginia. Don't you dare. Don't you blow it.

They're here with me. That should speak louder than any words that could come out of their mouths. They've put everything on hold to come with me. That pushes the bounds of daughterly duty. And for now, it will have to suffice.

Don't be greedy, Virginia.

As the car hums along the highway, I think about all the things I have to tell them, but I have to do it right. I can't just dump it on them all at once.

Where to start?

From the beginning, I suppose.

But before I begin, I flip open the vanity mirror on the back of the sun visor and push my sunglasses up on top of my head to check my makeup. I'm conscious of keeping concealer on that nasty bruise so I don't look like too much of a monster. As I'm thinking about how I'll start, I'm just about to grab my pocketbook to get the tube of that good Estée Lauder concealer Summer gave me, when I catch a glimpse of her in the backseat. She's got her eyes closed and her head's resting in that place where the seat and the car door meet. Her head's tipped at an angle that accentuates the pretty line of her cheekbones.

"Summer? Are ya comfortable, sugar?"

She doesn't answer me.

I glance at Skye. "Is she asleep?"

"I don't know, Mama. I suppose if she were awake she would've answered you."

I glance back, trying to figure out if she's playing possum or not. Either way, she doesn't look very comfortable with her head against the door like that and her hurt foot in that boot doohickey hanging off the seat.

"We should have brought a cushion or something to prop her foot up on so she'd be more comfortable."

Skye doesn't answer me.

I undo my seat belt and take off my jacket so I can ball it up and put it under Summer's foot.

"Mama, what are you doing?" Skye sounds annoyed. "Put your seat belt back on. If I have to stop quick, you'll go flying right through the windshield."

"Nonsense. You just keep your eyes on the road and worry about your drivin' instead of fussing over me and you won't need to stop quick."

I turn around and kneel and try to slide Summer's big ol' boot onto the seat so I can put my jacket under it.

"Ow! Ginny, what are you doing?"

Skye merges the car off the highway onto the shoulder of the road and stops. I have to grab the headrest to keep from toppling backward.

"What did you do that for?" I turn around and plant my bottom in the seat.

"Mama, I told you to turn around and sit down. I

can't drive with you climbing all over the car. For God's sake, you're worse than my kids." She adds under her breath, "When they were toddlers."

"Hey, missy, I don't appreciate that. And for the record, you didn't say anything about not climbing all over the car. You said if you had to stop quick, I'd go flying right through the windshield. I see that you were trying to prove that point."

"Well, there you go," says Skye. "Just be glad I didn't have to *really* slam on the brakes."

She picks up her cell phone, which is lying out on the console beneath the radio and checks it for probably the twentieth time.

"Are you expecting a call?" I ask.

She flips it shut and sets it down. "No, I am not. Now, put on your seat belt and let's get back on the road. I want to make it as far as Jackson, Mississippi, tonight and I don't want to get in there too late."

Cars whiz by. The interstate is pretty busy, even for a Saturday. "Just hold on a minute." I turn around again and pick up my jacket. I dropped it when Skye stopped. "I want to give Summer my jacket to put under her foot."

Summer swats me away. "Ginny, I don't want your

jacket. I'm fine just like this. But thank you, though. Now turn around like Skye asked you to."

I don't know why it hurts my feelings. It's stupid really, but it does. Maybe it's because I want everything to go so well. I take a deep breath and turn around and buckle myself in, reminding myself that I should be proud that my twins are strong, opinionated women. I just wish they'd cut me a little bit of slack.

As I silently fume off my hurt feelings, the soft whir of the car lulls my mind back in time to the last road trip I took through these parts with my girls. We were traveling this same route, only headed the opposite direction—away from Springvale. That bus couldn't get me far enough away, fast enough.

It was so long ago and not nearly under such agreeable circumstances, but the details are etched into my mind like an ugly mar on a beautiful mahogany table.

I check the mirror and see Summer is awake.

I wonder where to start. With the bus trip or back a few years? The story's a might bit more complicated than it seems on the surface. There are layers that I can't peel back all at once.

I take a deep breath before I dive in.

"I'll bet y'all never knew I went to nurses training, did you?"

"You went to college?" Skye asks. I'm relieved that her tone is softer than it was before.

"Yes, I did. On a full-ride scholarship."

"When did you graduate?" Skye says.

"Well, that's just it. I didn't graduate. I had to leave before I could finish."

"Why? What happened?" Summer asks.

I hesitate, clear my throat. Hmm, how to put this. "Money was scarce. You know my daddy died when I was fifteen. He didn't have much insurance—just enough to keep the house and put a little food on the table. Your grandma managed money with an iron fist. I had to hand it to her. You know the old saying about squeezing a nickel so hard the buffalo shits? Well, I think it originated with your Grandma Ina. She could stretch the budget further than anyone I ever knew. You see, I was at Florida State University—"

"Mama, you went to FSU?" Skye's jaw is all but dragging the floor. "I went to that school for four years and you never bothered to tell me?"

Uh-oh. She's mad again. Well, *irritated* is more the word. I knew this would happen, but it's part of it, so I just have to trudge on through.

"I suppose I never mentioned it because I ended up dropping out before I even finished the first semester. It's almost like it doesn't even count. I was afraid my being such a flake might have a negative impact when you were wanting to get in."

Summer leans forward. "You had a full-ride scholarship and you dropped out? What happened? Why'd you quit?"

"I got pregnant with you girls, and I ended up having to go home."

"Oh, great, blame it on us." Summer's joking, but I hear a hint of truth in her voice.

"Why didn't you go back later and finish?" Skye asks.

"You know how it is once you have kids. Skye, tell your sister how it is."

"It's difficult to have much time to do anything for yourself."

"Hence the reason I never had children." Summer's voice floats like a cat's purr. In the vanity mirror, I watch her stretch languidly and lounge against the backseat. Very felinelike, indeed.

I think of Nick and his boy, and I'm tempted to tell her that I didn't think I was maternal, either. Now, at age fifty-eight, I know my babies were the best thing that ever happened to me. It wasn't an easy path to this place of contentment. God, I don't know what would have become of me if not for my girls. I probably wouldn't be alive today.

"Yep, those was different times. So after I delivered you two, I had no choice but to go home to your grandma."

"Wait a minute, I thought you always said you were living in a commune when you conceived us." Summer leans forward again and braces her elbows on the backs of the two front seats. "What happened to all that free-sex, love-the-one-you're-with mumbo jumbo?"

I catch a whiff of her perfume, a nice blend of floral and spice. I'll have to remember to ask her what kind it is. Later, not right now.

"Well, I *did* live in a convent, *um*, just not right then. You were definitely conceived while I was flunking out of FSU."

"So you flunked? That's what happened to your scholarship?"

"If you must know, yes. That's what happened. It was an exciting time for a young girl who'd never been away from home."

"So what about the commune?"

"Just be patient. I'll get to that soon enough. All the threads of the story come together in the end."

"Oh," Summer quips from the backseat. "So mysterious."

"You just watch yourself, smarty-pants. There's not a thing mysterious about it." I turn and wink at her to keep the mood light. I'm pleased when she winks back. "After I delivered you, I went home to your Grandma Ina's house and when she discovered I'd gotten knocked up she nearly beat the tar out of me. I don't know what bothered her the most—that I'd had you on my own without telling her, or the pregnancy itself.

"She lived out on an old farm road. The closest neighbor was at least a mile away and Mother kept to herself anyway—not many friends—so it wasn't like she had to explain away the situation to anyone.

For those who did come around, she'd just say that my husband was away."

I can't help but shake my head thinking about it.

"But in all fairness to her, once she got over the shock, she loved you two like you were her own."

The girls are quiet and I can't quite read their expressions—Skye looks pensive, staring straight ahead at the road. In the mirror I can see Summer frowning in the backseat. I'm glad I have on these sunglasses so I can watch them without their knowing it.

"Yep, she sure enough loved you two. But she never could find it in her heart to forgive me for bringing you into the world. To tell you the truth, I think she rued the day that *I* came into the world. We never did have a very good relationship, but that's a whole different can of worms.

"Not a day went by that she didn't make me pay for my mistake until finally I decided I had to get the heck out of there. It was that bad. But I was barely in the frame of mind to take care of myself, much less two tiny babies. So I left y'all in your Grandma Ina's care."

Skye glances at me and I can see the wheels turning. "How long were you gone?"

"Three years. You know how kids are. I was a baby with two babies."

Summer

It's strange finding out all this information about someone who seemed to be an open book your entire life. I can't quite figure out where she's going with all this, but I suppose time will tell.

"I know we had some rough times when you were little and I'm sorry for that and sometimes I just hate myself for it. I really do."

Ginny sighs and stares straight ahead out the windshield. "I suppose the burning question is what could've made a mama treat her sweet babies like that?"

"I try not to dwell on it." The words sound a little more flippant than I intend. "But I have wondered what possessed you."

"Possessed." Ginny hisses the word. "Ha—now, that's a good word for it. I was sure enough possessed by something bigger and uglier than me. It might explain *that time*—you know, that time I had to...

leave. If I hadn't gone, who knows what might've happened. I want you to know, I'm not makin' excuses for myself." She looks at Skye then me in the mirror. "But you might understand me better once you know."

Skye tenses her shoulder muscles, lets them drop.

I hear a strange note in Ginny's voice. A nuance. But it's there. "After I had you girls, life with Ina was unbearable. I was nineteen years old and the longer I stayed in Springvale the more I felt as if I were going to go out of my ever-lovin' head.

"Y'all were the colickiest babies. I swear you must've cried nonstop the first three months of your life. I was going crazy, you fussin' nonstop, Mother being so darned hateful. I couldn't do anything right and she let me know about it in no uncertain terms."

Ginny pauses. A darkness washes over her. She looks from Skye to me.

"This is going to sound a little crazy, but all along, I kept hearing these…these voices. Telling me to do awful things."

"Like what?" Skye demands, her nose wrinkled.

"Kill myself and take y'all with me."

There's a pregnant pause, and at first I think she's

joking or being dramatic. She has such a flair for it. But there's something in her voice that sends a chill through me.

"At least I had enough sense to get the heck away before I harmed you. Mother doted on you. She was *good* to you, but she never let me forget that you were conceived in sin."

"Whoa, wait a sec." I hold up my hand, hoping to get a word in. "You're saying voices were telling you to *kill* us. As in dead?"

She nods so nonchalantly that it gives me the creeps.

"Okay, stop the car," I say. "I'm getting out."

"Oh, hush up. I'm not going to kill you now."

"Oh, thank God. I feel *so* much better. How about you, Skye?"

"Mmm-hmm."

Ginny moistens her lips. "Hear me out. The only chance I had to save myself and you was to get out from under my mother. So I left her house, but I left you in your grandma's care and went back to Florida thinking once I had some peace, I could get my life on track, the craziness would stop and I could come get you.

"And once I was out from under my mother, my outlook improved dramatically.

"I went back to Tallahassee thinking I was going to conquer the world. Maybe I wouldn't even bother with nurses training. I could be a doctor—that would show her.

"Only problem was, I'd lost my scholarship. I was so preoccupied with being pregnant—wondering what I was going to do once I couldn't hide my predicament anymore. Remember, those were different times. Even as liberated as people were about sex, they didn't look kindly upon a girl who'd gotten herself in trouble. That was still taboo. Oh, and I suffered such horrible morning sickness, half the time I couldn't even drag myself out of bed, let alone go to class. Well, long story short, I didn't even withdraw from my courses. I just stopped going. When I went back a year later, they wouldn't reinstate the scholarship."

I hate to admit it, but I'm perversely fascinated by this secret side of my mother. I look at Skye, but I can't read her.

"I wasn't going to let that stop me. Oh, no, no. I'd work my way through college. I had so much energy I didn't even need to sleep. I got a job wait-ressing. The tips were good, and after I'd saved up enough, I marched back over to that admissions office and plunked down the money and told them to forget nurses training, enroll me in premed.

"It was midsemester. So of course they couldn't let me in. And then the strangest thing began to happen. I started believing certain people wanted me out of Tallahassee, that my mother had sent these people to watch me and arrange for them to deny me reenter-ing school. I truly believed she was determined to make life so hard on me that I *had* to go home."

Skye makes a *pish* noise. "Mama, that's crazy."

"I know, darlin'. I know. And it gets even crazier. Just you listen. By that time, I'd lost my job and had spent almost all the money I'd saved. I believed Mother had arranged it so that no one in Tallahas-see would hire me. She'd systematically set out to ruin my life."

"Oh, come on." Skye rolls her eyes, but Ginny carries on undaunted.

"I wasn't about to go back to Springvale. I wasn't strong enough to face Mother, and I wasn't about to trust myself to care for you two.

"Not with the voices—one minute they were telling me to kill you, the next they were saying Mother was going to kill me once she got me home. Who knows, maybe she would have. Sometimes it seemed she was crazier than me."

Skye glances at her. "Are you saying you were hearing voices like you're hearing me sitting here talking to you?"

Ginny looks thoughtful, as if she's trying to figure out how to explain. "Not exactly. It was more a feeling I had. Inside my head. Like an impulse driving me to the edge."

She presses her hands to her temples.

"Good," I say. "For a minute, I was afraid you were going to tell us you were one of those crazy people who wander around talking to themselves."

I laugh, but Ginny leans her head back on the headrest. I see Skye's eyes in the rearview mirror. They look as if she's having a hard time digesting the story.

"I was in bad shape, sleeping on people's couches—whoever would take me in. This lasted about four months. Until finally someone—Lord, I can't even remember the gal's name—told me about a commune down in Cocoa Beach. I could get room and board in exchange for my helping with the gardening and chores around the compound. So I hitched a ride there, hoping against hope that it would give me a chance to get back on my feet and figure out what to do next.

"But it all seemed so hopeless. Even getting out of bed in the morning was too much for me to bear— much worse than the morning sickness. Something stronger than me took hold and was dragging me under. I decided that the only way to end the madness was to…"

She shakes her head as if the memory is too painful. She sucks in a deep breath and bows her head.

"I tried to kill myself. I tried to slit my wrists."

"Mama!" Skye gasps.

Oh, dear God, Ginny…

Skye's arm is resting on the console and Ginny takes her hand.

I ball my hands into fists so tight my nails bite into my palms.

"A guy named Paul found me and got me to the hospital in the nick of time. If there's a bright side to this, nearly killing myself is probably what saved my life."

Skye gasps. "Oh, Mama. I had no idea. Why didn't you tell us this before?"

Ginny shrugs, shakes her head as if she's bewildered by the question. "I guess I was a little bit ashamed." She chokes on the words and steadies herself. "I was diagnosed with manic depression—Well, that's what it was called back then. Today they call it bipolar disorder. I spent the better part of a year in a mental hospital, where they put me on medication and got me straightened out."

We're quiet. I don't know what to say to that. Obviously Skye doesn't, either.

"So there you have it. Your mama's a certified nutcase. But I guess you knew that already. Didn't ya?"

She laughs, but it sounds as if she's manufactured the humor in her voice.

"So what happened?" I ask.

"The rest of the story goes just as I told you before. I called my mother to tell her I was coming to get my babies. Land, by then y'all was three years old. I was finally healthy."

She sighs.

"I missed you like I was missing a piece of my soul. Don't you see? I was sick. But even through the worst of it I still loved you and wanted what was best for you. I only went off my meds one time." She holds up her index finger for emphasis. "I was feeling so good, so normal I thought I didn't need it anymore. That's when—"

"We were eleven." There's a hint of contempt in Skye's voice. "You went off and left us again."

Ginny's gaze locks with Skye's and there's a flash of something in my mother's expression. Guilt? Remorse? Horror? Maybe all rolled into one.

Ginny lowers her eyes, her mouth pressed into a thin line and then she shakes herself back into recognizable form.

"I went to get help and you know I was better to you after that, wasn't I? I never went off my meds again."

Neither Skye nor I answer.

"A few years later I met Chester and I got pregnant with Jane. I thought about not having that baby. After all I'd put you through, it just didn't seem right. But the more I thought about it, the more I realized it was exactly what I had to do."

She pauses just long enough to swipe at her tears with the back of her thumb.

"I had to do it because I thought that somehow

I could have this child and make up for the rotten job I did with you two. I loved Chester and I wanted to go back and do it over—the right way. This was my chance."

She's talking too fast and I'm having a hard time figuring out exactly how having another baby could *make up for* what she did to us. Then I realize it's about easing her own troubled conscience. Anger floats to the surface like the bubbles in a pot left simmering too long. I can't help myself. I lean forward and the words spill out.

"So you spoiled Jane rotten and look how great things turned out."

She turns to look at me, a flash of surprise in her eyes, as if she'd never considered that before.

"I know how it must've seemed, darlin', but there's more to it than that."

She closes her eyes as if she's gathering strength.

"You might as well know this, too. Jane started showing signs of bipolar right after Chester died. They say the first episode's usually triggered by a traumatic event." She looks deflated, spent. "Well, she was fourteen and with her daddy dying, I figured her black moods were due to Chester's death on top of the normal haywire of teenage hormones. I suppose I didn't want to believe anything permanent was wrong. But after she ran away that first time, I had to face facts. I got her to a doctor and got her on medication to straighten her out."

Ginny sniffs, picks up her tissue and blots the corners of her eyes.

"She wouldn't stay on her meds and that's when everything went downhill."

"Ginny, why didn't you tell us about Jane's condition?" I ask.

Her shoulders rise and fall on a sigh. "She was embarrassed by her illness, when she'd even admit anything was wrong. The one time she admitted she was sick, she made me swear I wouldn't tell anyone. Especially not the two of you. She idolized you. Her older sisters. So successful, so sure of yourselves.

"I had to honor that promise I made to her."

"But I suppose it entered into your mind that by telling us about Jane, you'd have to tell us about you, too?" I say.

Ginny shrugs. Her expression says she doesn't appreciate this remark.

"Is bipolar disease hereditary?" Skye asks.

"Yes, darlin', it is."

Skye gives Ginny a hard look.

"Mama, that means all three of my children could suffer from the disease. You should have told me about this before I had kids."

Ginny reaches out to her, but Skye pulls away. "Honey, it's probably best you didn't know—"

"Don't you even try to tell me what's best for me, for my family."

Skye flips on her signal and merges off onto a rest stop exit.

"I have a sixteen-year-old girl who hates my guts half the time and that's only when she's not busy crying over some other perceived wrong someone else has done to her."

Skye pulls into a parking space, breaking to a jerky stop. She blinks at our mother as if words are logjammed in her throat, but finally manages, "Mama, *how* could you keep this from us?"

On a frustrated wail, my sister storms out of the car.

Skye

Okay, so it's bipolar disorder. It's not AIDS or terminal cancer. But still, the way Becky's been acting and the shock of this side of Mama that she's kept locked away in her mental vault all these years, it *does* take a minute—or ten to digest.

I had to get out of there. My head was spinning, the car was closing in and for a minute I really thought I was going to lose it.

I guess I did. Sort of.

I walk back to the car. Summer and Mama are still sitting inside.

"Oh, Mama." *Dragging us all the way out here in the middle of nowhere and telling us something like this. Why didn't you do this years ago?*

When I open the car door, Mama dumps a rush of reasons in my lap.

"Darlin', I understand how upset you must be and I'm sure it's shocking and I didn't tell you before you got married, because knowing you, it would've probably stopped you from having kids and let me ask you something, after holding your sweet babies in your arms, would you really want to go back and *not* have them for fear of a mental disorder that may or may not affect them and even if it does it can be controlled by medication? Could you imagine your life without those children?"

My mind is whirling. I stare at her as she draws in air like she's yoga-breathing.

We drive for three hours in relative silence. It gives me time to think. Time to sort things out in my mind. Like how being bipolar affected Mama's life and how frightening it must have been before she knew what was wrong with her.

By the time we get to Mobile, Alabama, just after noon, I feel a little more human again. I steer the car off I-10 into the crowded, gravel parking lot of Bea's Diner.

It's a homey little restaurant with flowering window boxes, rocking chairs on the front porch and a Native American gift shop, which seems a little incongruent for this area, but I thought I might be able to find a fun souvenir for the kids.

"Is this all right?" I ask.

"Anything's fine with me," says Summer. "I want a smoke."

"Honey, we can eat anywhere you want." Mama's voice is soft and sweet. Despite how mad I was at her—actually, I think I was shocked more than mad—I want to digest this and get to the other side of it. I suppose she had her reasons for not telling us. Obviously, reasons that seemed valid to her.

At least she told us.

Better late than never. I guess.

I'm glad Mama and Summer have agreed to Bea's over the typical fast-food joints that populate the exit. Those places never seem very clean. All we need is a bad case of botulism to make this road trip complete. This one might not be any better, but I can't help but think if Bea (or Bea's proxy) would bother to set out flowers she would keep a decent kitchen.

Before I get out of the car, I unplug my phone from the charger and check to make sure it's on. Cameron hasn't called. I knew he'd be mad at me for going with Mama, but if he wanted me to arrange care for the kids, he should have rung me back like I asked him to rather than giving me the silent treatment.

I consider calling him one more time, giving him the benefit of the doubt—maybe he didn't get the message. It's more that maybe he didn't care enough to check his messages. I tuck the phone inside my purse. The ball's in his court. If he can't find two minutes in his busy schedule to call me, well, I suppose he won't have time to pick up another message from me, either.

Mama and I go in and get a table while Summer has a smoke outside. She already had the cigarette and lighter in her hand as I helped her out of the car. I have to hand it to her—she's been a good sport about not insisting we stop for cigarette breaks. Maybe she'll see she's not as dependent on those nasty things as she thinks.

Inside the diner there's a *please seat yourself* sign, and Mama slides into the only free booth. The place is fairly busy. It looks decent and the smells coming from the kitchen are inviting.

Mama takes two plastic-covered menus from the stack propped between the wall and the chrome napkin holder and hands one to me. She looks tired and the makeup she's been dabbing under her eye all morning is caked and turning the bruise a strange shade of gray. The only thing worse than botulism would be if we got out in the middle of nowhere and she had a setback. I whisper a silent prayer that she'll be okay and remind myself that the doctor wouldn't have cleared her to go if he was the least bit uncertain she was fine.

"Are you feeling okay?" I ask.

She smiles. The film of concealer moves. "Couldn't be better. How about you, honey?"

"I'm fine. Just a little surprised is all."

She studies my face as if she's trying to decide whether I am just that—fine.

"And for the record," I say. "Knowing what I know now, if I had the chance to go back and *not* have my kids—I'd have them."

She smiles.

I reach across the table and smooth out her concealer.

She puts her hand over mine. "What are you doing?"

"Fixing your makeup. In this light it looks different."

She pulls a compact from her purse and checks for herself. "Lord have mercy, I look terrible."

"You look fine, Mama. Don't worry about it."

She returns the compact to her purse, but pulls out her sunglasses and slides them on. I roll my eyes and regret starting this whole thing.

"Now you look silly, wearing your shades inside. Mama, take them off. You're drawing more attention to yourself wearing them in here."

She opens her menu but leaves the sunglasses in place.

So vain. Always has been.

It reminds me of the Greek myth about Narcissus, who fell in love with his own reflection. Well, except that Narcissus was a man. Oh, and I suppose that because Mama's always been proud of her appearance doesn't mean she's in love with her looks.

I don't know what I was thinking.

Jane got Mama's looks. Summer and I don't look anything like her. We're taller, larger boned.

Different. I guess we look like our daddy and I wonder if Mama gets any hint of which one he was when she looks at us?

I've also wondered if Mama's being so petite didn't play into Summer's obsession with her weight. For me, well, let's just call it a losing battle.

My stomach growls.

I scan the lunch specials and decide on a cheeseburger with the works and fries because I'm starving and the aroma of frying burgers is too heavenly to resist.

I'll start my diet after I get home.

That settled, I snap the menu shut and return it to its place against the wall.

"What are you going to have?" I ask her.

She's still studying the choices. "*Mmm*…I think I'll just have the chef salad. I don't want anything too heavy since we'll be sitting so much today."

I pick up the menu and look at it again. For a minute, I consider ordering the salad, too. It would be more in line with my Atkins plan, but it wouldn't be nearly as satisfying as the cheeseburger.

Nah, I'll stick with my original choice, I decide, glancing around the diner. The place is a throwback to the sixties (maybe even the fifties). From the looks of the fixtures it might even be the genuine article: booths with red leatherette benches, gray Formica-topped tables, snack bar with an army of dingy chrome stools standing at attention in front of it, a pie rack on the counter with a plastic cover that's so cloudy I can't make out what kind of pie they're serving and a jukebox in the far corner playing the song "Dust in the Wind." The music proves the place is authentic. If they were trying to look like an old diner they'd have nothing but fifties-sixties music in the jukebox. Not this seventies standard.

The song makes me think of Nick and I wonder why. Because he and Summer are back in touch?

Did we dance to it at the prom? Maybe it was one of those random songs playing on the radio at no special time that sticks in your mind for some unknown reason? When we dated, the song would've been a few years old. Who knows? All I know is it reminds me of him, but it doesn't matter.

Though I didn't always feel that way.

Summer's shenanigan of stealing Nick away from me nearly shoved a permanent wedge between us. It's not that he chose her over me—I mean, come on, I found someone much better suited for me. Nick obviously loved her (even if they didn't last—what a surprise). It was the principle of the matter. Women who care about their sisters *do not* sleep with said sister's boyfriend. It took a lot to get over a betrayal like that.

It was a long time ago. Water under the bridge, as far as I'm concerned. Because what is life without a forgiving heart? That's what I've been trying to master—having a forgiving heart.

I think of Mama and Grandma Ina. After Mama took us away from her, we never saw Grandma Ina again. Mama always chalked it up to a feud they'd had. Little did I know.

Summer and I were twenty-five when Grandma died. We were both too wrapped up in making our own ways to even think of making amends with a grandmother who'd never been in our lives and seemingly didn't care.

Learning that we lived with her for the first three years of our lives feels strange. If you think about it, the first few years of life are the most formative. Some psychologists believe those years lay the foundation upon which personality is built.

A million questions sweep through my mind. For some strange reason, I can't form them into intelligible sentences. Maybe I'm afraid of the answers.

So I ask her nothing.

For now.

Just as well. A petite young woman in a tight-fitting pink waitress uniform comes over to take our order. Her black name tag reads Misty. She's chomping on gum and has her order pad and pen poised and ready to go.

"What'll ya have?" Her accent is so thick it makes people in Tallahassee sound bland.

"We're waiting for someone," Mama says. "What

do you suppose is keeping Summer? Should I go out and see about her?"

I shake my head.

"She's smoking, Mama. And I suspect she's having more than one to make up for lost time. Why don't you order your food, then you can go out and spur her along if you want. We can't stay here too long. We still have a good four hours ahead of us before we reach Jackson, Mississippi, where we're staying tonight."

We give the waitress our order and she hasn't as much as walked away from our table when Summer walks through the door.

"I was just about ready to come get you," Mama says.

The look on Summer's face as she slides in next to me conveys that wouldn't have been a good idea.

"What are you going to eat, sweetie?" Mama smiles and thrusts a menu across the table at her as if nothing's wrong.

Summer waves it away. "Nothing."

"You've got to eat. All you had for breakfast was juice and coffee."

"My stomach's a little upset."

To get Mama off her back, she orders toast and a Diet Coke, but leaves most of the bread on her plate.

I, on the other hand, eat every last satisfying smidgen of my burger and fries.

After we finish, Summer goes outside for one last smoke, Mama goes to the bathroom and I have a look around the gift shop.

I pick up a little black change purse sewn with tiny colored beads. *Becky* is worked into the design, spelled out with black beads. Tracing the name with the pad of my index finger, I feel a pang of nostalgia. Not too many years ago my oldest would have been all over a little purse like this. We couldn't pass a gift shop without her begging to stop and go inside. She was in heaven in a place like this.

But now she wouldn't care anything about a cheap little remembrance from a place like this, especially a little purse with her name on it. My God, where did the years go? I feel kind of sad as I tuck the little wallet back into its place on the shelf, leaving it for another little Becky who will get excited over it.

But, if I'm bringing home gifts for Sydney and Cole, I'd better get something for her, too. I turn to look for something more appropriate and catch a glimpse of Mama beneath the sea of low-flying mobiles, wind chimes and dream catchers strung from the painted ceiling of the shop. It startles me how much she and Jane look alike. I wonder what shape Jane will be in when we find her.

The dream I had the night before last flashes in my mind and I blink it away. No. She's okay. Everything's going to be okay.

Mama walks up next to me and picks up a small drum covered with faux buckskin.

"Do you suppose Cole would like one of these?"

I shake my head. "Mama, he's twelve years old. If it doesn't run on batteries or electricity, he has no interest it."

She shrugs and holds it up for one last look. "You and Summer used to have one kind of like this. Do you remember?"

I shake my head no, but the memory comes flooding back as if I'd opened a box of forgotten treasures. Only now the riches that once were so shiny and new look old and tarnished and broken.

In my mind, I hear Mama saying, "This isn't any ol' drum, you know. It's magic. If you want something bad enough, all you have to do is place your wish in your heart and beat on this drum. The great spirits will grant you your wish. It's true. Just go ahead and try it."

Oh, Mama. How could you say such a thing to a little kid who wanted so desperately to believe in you? To a little kid who wanted a daddy like all the other kids she went to school with? What were you trying to do?

She smiles a sad smile, as if she can read my mind and, before she sets it back on the shelf, she closes her eyes and beats the drum.

Just four soft, simple beats and then she tucks it away.

Summer comes into the shop and walks over to the display of drums. Picks up one. "Hey, Skye, we used to have one of these. Do you remember?"

I ignore her and walk over to the dream catchers. I buy two. One for each of my girls—orange for Becky, because it's her favorite color, and purple to match Sydney's room. For Cole, I select a brightly colored mobile.

Funny how Cole's having outgrown a drum doesn't disable me the way Becky's growing up does. She worries me more.

Not that I love Cole any less. I suppose it has something to do with Becky being my firstborn and the way she's been pulling away lately. I trace the web pattern on the dream catcher. I suppose I've always felt there was something *different* about Becky. She's perfectly normal, does well in school, but there's something—almost fragile about her. Something only a mother could discern.

I think of all that Mama poured out in the car and shiver. Summer comes to stand with me in line. She's holding one of those drums.

"Why are you buying that?" I ask.

"I thought Nick's little boy might like it."

"That's sweet, but just don't fill his head with all that nonsense about it being a wishing drum. That only breeds disappointment in little kids. Don't you remember?"

"Oh, Skye, lighten up. It was fun. If you can't believe in magic when you're young, when will you believe in it?"

My jaded sister closes her eyes and raps lightly on the drum. Just for the fun of it, I decide if I were to wish, I'd wish that Becky would be okay, that Cameron would call and…oh, what else? That I could retire the ceiling-monster dream and Jane would be okay.

I pluck the drumstick from Summer's hand and give four light taps on the tom-tom—one for each wish.

Feeling a little sad as I step up to the wrap stand and lay down the merchandise I want to buy, I pluck three bottles of Diet Coke out of a big, round, ice-filled cooler that's sitting next to the cash register and wait for the cashier to give me my total.

Just as he's handing me my change, the little waitress in the pink nylon uniform comes rushing into the gift shop. "Oh, I'm so glad you're still here. You left your cell phone on the table."

A mixture of icy-hot panic and relief rush through me as I take it from her. I shove the phone into my purse where it should have been in the first place rather than sitting out on the table—as if watching it was going to make Cameron call. Thanking the girl profusely, I pull a five-dollar bill from my wallet and try to hand it to her.

"I can't accept this," she says.

"Please, take it." I press the bill into her palm. "You really saved me by finding it and taking the initiative to come in here and find me. Please."

Graciously, she accepts the money and tucks the bill in her pocket.

Once we're back on the road, Mama says, "Well, I certainly feel refreshed. Nothing like a good stretch and a meal to revive the soul. A little shopping never hurt, either."

"Mama, do me a favor? Get my phone from my purse and plug it into the charger for me?"

"Sure, darlin'." She pulls out the phone and holds it up to look at it. "Funny, I didn't hear the phone ring. Did you?"

"No, it didn't ring."

"Well, it must have sometime—maybe while you left it sitting on the table? Because it says here, one missed call."

My heart nearly lurches out of my chest.

She hands me the phone. I glance at the number and my heart sinks back into my chest when I see the missed call is Cameron.

"I guess that call you were waiting for finally came through?" says Mama.

Thinking about the silly wish I made on the tom-tom that Summer bought, I break the number one rule that I impose on Becky and I check my voice mail while I'm driving.

Just this once.

But there's no message.

And of course there is no magic. There are only coincidences.

CHAPTER 12

Summer

The four-hour drive to the Jackson, Mississippi, Red Roof Inn where we're spending the night seems to take an eternity. It's endless flat, rural four-lane highway bordered by one cow pasture running into the next. By the time we get to Jackson, it seems like a cosmopolitan city.

It's been a trying day. My foot hurts, I have a headache from reading the map (I get carsick if I read in a moving vehicle) and I'm exhausted—emotionally and physically. We haven't spent this much time together in such close quarters in, God, at least twenty years. Now I remember why.

Skye's bossy and Ginny talks compulsively. That three-hour stretch where Skye was mad at her was pure heaven because our mother didn't utter a word.

But after lunch it was all downhill. Is it really neces-
sary to comment on every bovine, barn and billboard
for riverboat gambling we pass? When she's not doing
that she's arguing with Skye about letting her share
the driving.

"It's too much for one person to do all this drivin',
darlin'. Let me help."

"No, Mama. I prefer to drive. You just sit right there
and look at the map and tell me what my next exit is."

"But I'm not a good navigator, I can't make heads
nor tails of this thing."

"Well, then, it's time you learned."

And on and on and on. Until I finally volunteer
to be the navigator, leaving Ginny free to read the
billboards to us.

Note to self: buy earplugs for the drive tomorrow.

I'm sure they think I'm cranky. I *am* cranky. My leg
hurts. My head hurts. My ears hurt from the prattle.
When you put bossy, chatty and surly together in
one small SUV, it's a volatile combination.

At the registration desk, Skye asks for a double
room, but I'm just not up to it. I need some space.

"If you don't mind," I say, "I'm going to get my
own room."

I brace for a snipe from Skye about how if money is scarce it's foolish to pay extra when we can all sleep in one room for one night, but she says, "Me, too. This is my room."

Ginny doesn't bat an eye, just steps up to the desk and whips out her platinum American Express. "All three rooms on one bill, please."

"Mama, no."

"Really, Ginny, I can pick up the tab for mine."

"Hush. I've dragged you all out here. I'll pay the bill. This isn't exactly a pleasure cruise nor is it the Taj Mahal. So step back and afford me this one pleasure."

We do and we arrange to meet back in the lobby fifteen minutes later to go to dinner. Ginny's changed into a low-cut, neon-orange sundress and mesh over a jacket with real shells and a seashore design woven in silver, gold and white thread. She has strappy gold sandals on her feet. The ensemble's a tad gaudy—not that she's ever been a fashion plate, but she never dressed like this before Chester Hamby. I'm sure it was expensive because it screams Palm Beach resort wear. She's even dabbed on some thick opalescent lipstick. All she's missing is the deep tan, but she never was a sun worshipper, and she has a glowing peaches-and-cream complexion to show for it.

Skye and I are still wearing the same clothes we've traveled in all day.

The desk clerk, who is probably in his early fifties, eyes Ginny appreciatively as he directs us to a moderately-priced steakhouse about a mile down the road. The place was Ginny's choice.

"I want to treat y'all to a nice meal since you were so good to come with me on this trip."

Who are we to argue with that?

The restaurant is dimly lit with lots of dark wood and amber-glass partitions. The faint strains of a country song play over the sound system, and the place smells of sizzling steaks and a slightly sour scent I can't readily identify.

Vinaigrette? Cheap wine?

The restaurant's crowded, but luckily we don't have to wait to be seated. The hostess leads us to the center of the dining room to a four-top with a white tablecloth that's covered by a piece of Plexiglas. A bud vase with a dusty, fake red rose stands in the center surrounded by a votive candle and plastic salt and pepper shakers.

"I hope the food's good," says Ginny, looking around. "I'm hungry."

She sniffs the air. "Mmm-mmm, sure does smell good. How 'bout a drink, girls?"

She signals the server and orders a Scotch and soda. Skye and I order glasses of red wine.

"Why don't y'all go on and get yourself a bottle? Come on. Don't be shy. You order whatever y'all want."

"No, Mama, really. One glass is my limit. Especially since I'm driving."

"And I shouldn't drink too much since I'm taking pain medicine for my leg."

"Bring them a bottle of whatever that is they've ordered."

We make small talk about insignificant things, because I think we are both wary to bring up the bipolar discussion we had this morning. Personally, I hope we can just have a nice, low-key dinner, go back to our rooms and go to sleep without incident.

By the time the server brings our meals, Ginny's downed two cocktails and has moved on to "tasting" the bottle of wine she ordered for Skye and me. She decides it pairs quite nicely with her fillet mignon and pours herself a full glass.

"I've been thinking a lot about that old saying *you can't go home again*," she says. "Have you heard it before?"

I remember my thoughts the day I arrived. Ironic. God, am I becoming my mother? I'm tempted to make a joke of it, but Skye nods as she cuts a piece of her prime rib.

"It's a book by Thomas Wolfe. I read it when I was in high school."

Ginny shakes her head and smiles in wonder. "You are so smart." As if she remembers she's leaving me out, she touches my hand. "I'm so proud of how you *both* turned out. I don't know much about books or fashion as you two do, but I think what ol' Tom Wolfe—is that his name? Well, whoever he is, what he says is true."

"That assumes the place you're returning to was home to begin with."

The ice cubes clink as she lifts her glass to her lips and takes a slow pull off the dregs of her cocktail.

"Is that how you feel, Summer, about coming back to Dahlia Springs?"

I raise one shoulder, let it fall. What am I supposed to say? That it's the last place on earth I want to be?

"I feel for ya, darlin', because I'm not thrilled about going back to Springvale. Too many bad memories. Too many ghosts that have been weighing me down since you two were born."

The server comes by and refills our water glasses. She raises her empty Scotch glass to him, signaling for another.

"You girls are so good to me." She shakes her head sadly. There's a certain look in her eye—a sort of soft-focus dreamy—that prompts Skye and me to exchange a glance.

The server delivers her fresh drink. She takes a long swallow of courage.

"There's one more thing I have to tell you. I'm telling you now because it has nothing to do with Jane." Her words are soft around the edges and her eyes have a glassy, faraway look.

One more thing? I shoot Skye a look. She sets down her fork.

"I guess I wasn't completely truthful when I told you I needed all three of my girls together before I could tell you what I needed to tell you. I'm afraid I'm a big coward and I needed to get you somewhere that you couldn't walk away from me—at least until you hear me out. I hope you'll forgive me for that on top of everything else." She grabs my hand because it's on the table and Skye's forearm because her hands are in her lap. "Promise me you won't leave me out here in the middle of nowhere. Not when your sister needs us to come get her? Promise me you won't leave me after that, either?"

Skye shakes out of her grip and Ginny squeezes my hand tighter. The strength in her grip surprises me. *So this is the reason you dragged us all the way out here. Buy us dinner, ply us with wine. Get us all softened up and then stick it to us.*

Oh, yeah, I can see the headlight on the Ginny train barreling down the track straight for us, ready to mow us down. I don't know if I have enough energy to get out of the way.

She does that to you. Sucks every ounce of energy right out of your body.

I shoot Skye another what-should-we-do? look.

My sister shifts in her chair. "Mama, I don't know if this is the place for this conversation. Why don't we ask for the check and go back to the motel so we can all get comfortable?"

"Nonsense, I'm fine right here and you're not finished with your meal. Go on now, eat and let me say what I've got to say before I lose my nerve."

Skye shrinks back into her chair and sips her wine. I push the mushrooms around on my plate.

"In the fall of sixty-six, when I left Springvale to study nursing at the university, as I told you, well, things happened. You know how sometimes even the best-laid plans don't work out like ya intend?"

Ginny pauses. A darkness washes over her. She looks from Skye to me, then at the flickering candle.

"Money was real scarce, remember how I told you I had to take a job? I was working as a maid at the governor's mansion. I was darn lucky to get that job. Nice working conditions. Good pay. I worked the night shift, which left my days free so I could attend classes. Lord, those were the days when I could get by on just a few hours' sleep. Now, I'm such a baby when it comes to my sleep."

She laughs. When she stops, she looks at us as if she just realized we weren't laughing, too.

"Everything seemed to be falling into place.

Work, school, I was out of my mother's house and doing quite fine on my own.

"She was dead-set against me going away. I told you that. Thought I couldn't make it on my own. Said I'd be back once my high-and-mighty ideas fizzled and dropped me on my ass."

She chuckles, but it's a sad sound. Shakes her head and stares at the candle in the center of the table.

"There weren't very many people in the governor's mansion at night. Just Governor Robert English and his wife. She was gone more than she was there.

"As part of my duties, I had to go through all the common areas of the house and empty the trash, make sure everything was presentable. Well, one night 'round midnight, Governor English walks into the library while I'm cleaning. I try to excuse myself so I can leave him undisturbed—we were instructed to drop everything if the governor or his family came in a room where we were cleaning. But he told me to stay and started talking to me while I worked. I was flattered that a man of his station had anything to say to the likes of me.

"He asked me about school and where I was from. And he listened when I talked, seemed genuinely interested. And, well, as time went on, he started appearing in the library every night 'round the same time."

Her voice is low and raw. She clears her throat and takes a long swallow of her Scotch. But she never takes her eyes off the candle.

"Keep in mind I was scarcely eighteen years old. Naive as a newborn kitten and just as starved for attention." She straightens a little. "I guess you might say I was a beauty. At least he used to tell me so.

"It was late nineteen sixty-six, and he was rich and powerful and so handsome. And used to getting *everything* he wanted. In that day, people looked the other way when faced with the dalliances of such a powerful man. Do you understand what I'm saying?"

She bites her lip for a minute. Neither Skye nor I utter a word.

"Robert was in his last term as governor, and everyone speculated he'd be the Republican candidate for the presidency. I was swept away by the romance of it all. I suppose on some level I fancied he was my ticket out of poverty. My mother would change her tune when she saw I was fixin' to marry a man who would be president. More than that, Robert was my white knight who'd ridden in to sweep me away. He was my dream come true. And he loved me."

"But Mama," Skye whispers, "he was married."

I'd been so engrossed in Ginny's story I hadn't noticed Skye's look of disgust. Sitting there with her lip curled and her arms crossed.

"I know, baby. I thought he was going to leave his wife and take me with him when he moved on to bigger things. What a handsome couple we'd make... I told you I was nothing more than a naive girl from the Ozarks. And everything changed when I told him I was pregnant. Not only did my handsome prince cut all lines of communication, he sent his men with money and a directive that I was to see a certain doctor who would 'take care of the situation.' The men told me if I didn't comply, I'd regret it."

There are tears in her eyes. She swipes at them, but they trickle down her cheeks like rain.

As she swallows the last of her Scotch, I shift in my chair as the possibility of where her story's going flushes through my veins like ice water.

"Mama?" Skye murmurs warily and I know by the tone of her voice she's drawing the same conclusion.

Ginny nods. "I couldn't terminate the pregnancy. I just couldn't give up my babies. You see, I loved you even then."

Holy sh— I've lost all feeling in my body and close my eyes against the shock.

"Are you telling us you've known all along who our father is, but you never bothered to tell us?" Skye spits the words like venom.

Ginny nods. "I couldn't. I—"

"You *lied* to us all these years, making us think you had no idea who our daddy was, while all along he was right there?" Skye scoots back her chair and leans forward, her palms braced on the edge of the table.

Ginny touches Skye's hand, but Skye yanks it away and knocks over her chair as she stands up and backs away from her.

"You lied to us, Mama!" she yells. People in the restaurant turn and stare as my sister walks out.

CHAPTER 13

Skye

After sitting in the car for ten minutes, resting my forehead on my hands on the steering wheel, I've calmed down enough to feel foolish for running out of the restaurant like I did.

I lift my head and look at the entrance of the steakhouse to see if they've come out yet. An older couple walks out and a family of five walks in, but no Mama and Summer.

"Mama."

Oh! I can't believe her. Dragging us all the way out here in the middle of nowhere and telling us something like this in a public place. It crosses my mind that the accident and coma were all staged to gain a sympathetic edge. To soften Summer and me

up so we'd willingly drive her four hundred miles just
so she could drop the bomb.

But common sense dictates she didn't stage it.
Nope, she simply took advantage of an opportunity
and used it to purge her guilty conscience.

I have a notion to leave Mama stranded high
and dry in Jackson, Mississippi. Just drive off
without her. She better be glad Summer's got a
broken foot.

Actually, even if she didn't have the broken foot,
I'm not sure I'd have the guts to do it.

And Mama knows that.

"Such a manipulator!"

Why are you letting her manipulate you? Cameron's
words echo in my head. He'll never let me hear the
end of this, once he starts speaking to me again. I
hate it when he's right.

I pound on the steering wheel and accidentally
honk the horn. Summer hobbles out into the night
with Mama, looking grim and drawn, at her side.

Good.

I hope she *has* been worrying that I drove off
and left her.

Summer looks stoic. I can't believe she can be so

calm in the face of all this. At least one of us is composed.

Mama starts talking the second she opens the car door. "Darlin', I understand how upset you must be. I'm sure it's shocking to—"

She doesn't even help Summer get in the car. Just keeps talking and talking.

I hop out to help Summer with her crutches.

"Skye, where are you going?" Mama's voice grows fainter until by the time I've circled to the front of the car I can't hear her at all.

When she realizes what I'm doing she gets out, too. "You have to understand, I have reasons for not telling you." She grabs at the crutches, but I yank back. "Your Grandma Ina demanded to know who your father was. She was hell-bent on finding him and making him marry me so my babies would have a name and a respectable life. But I couldn't tell her."

The way she keeps saying *my babies* irks me. I want to scream *You're talking about Summer and me*.

"She would have ruined everything. That's when I knew the only option I had was to tell her I didn't know the father's identity. She beat me, Skye, so brutally I almost died."

The words *Maybe it would have been better for all of us if you had died* knock at the door in my mind, but I fasten the dead bolt in my head, determined lock them out.

I shut Summer's door, and I don't even look at my mother as I walk back to the driver's side.

"Baby, please," she says when I get back in.

"Just be quiet, Mama. Stop talking long enough so I can hear myself think."

She has the decency to duck her head and nod.

I start the car and pull out of the parking lot in the direction of the motel. Glancing in the rearview mirror, I try to gauge Summer's reaction. But she's turned to the side staring out the rear window. I wonder what she and Mama talked about while they were alone inside the restaurant. Or *if* they talked. Where I explode, Summer has a tendency to shut down in the middle of a confrontation.

Mama's silent and so am I. Until I stop behind a line of traffic at a light on the highway.

Questions choke me. Why? Why? Why? I need to know. I want every last excuse she can come up with so I can feast on it like vulture on carrion.

"Why, Mama? Why now after all these years?"

She rolls her shoulders. "I know you're mad now," she murmurs. "But I just thought you needed to know."

"Don't you think this comes a little late?" says Summer, and I get some satisfaction hoping she's as furious as I am. "We needed our father when we were little girls, all the nights you left us alone in the apartment because you had to go to your waitress job—or whatever it was you did—because you couldn't afford a sitter. Why didn't you ask him to take responsibility for us when we really needed him?"

She dips her head and wrings her hands. Shadows fill the valleys of her cheekbones, accentuating them. "Robert English never loved me. He just took advantage of a naive country girl. His love was a paranoid delusion. In those days, the government didn't enforce child support the way they do now. I was just a sick, young girl and the way Robert's men threatened me, I *believed* they really would have killed us if they knew I went ahead and had you. With his political future at stake, he wasn't about to let a scandal keep him from the White House. I suppose it's small solace that he didn't win the election."

I wonder if that's supposed to be a joke, but no one laughs.

"If that was all a delusion, how do we know the entire affair wasn't imagined?" I say.

"Well, I do have two babies to show for it, don't I? I doubt that would happen in an imagined affair."

"Mama, you could have gotten pregnant by anyone, so don't give me that. I don't even know if I believe you."

Her demeanor transformed from intense remorse to steely seriousness in an instant. "I have been stable since you were eleven years old. Why after all these years would I invent something like this if it were not true? Robert English took advantage of me and then threw me away when he was done—"

"You've made playing the victim your life's work." Summer's voice cuts the air. "Haven't you, Ginny?"

I glance at Mama and, for the first time, I think she's at a loss for words. The light turns green, and when the traffic starts moving, I ease my foot down on the accelerator.

"Would it help if I told you how proud I am of you?"

I won't even dignify her comment with an answer. I half expect her to say her tough love is what got us where we are today. Maybe it is, because deep down we're all pretty screwed up.

"Just look at all that you've accomplished. Summer, you're modeling up in New York. Skye, you're married to a successful man and have three precious babies of your own."

My elbow's resting on the center console. As I turn into the parking lot of the Red Roof Inn, she reaches out to touch my arm, but I move before she can, gripping the steering wheel at ten and two. Her hand hovers in midair until, finally, she rests it in her lap.

"Skye, you always jumped right into mothering mode when I was gone, bossing Summer around, making sure y'all got your baths and were in bed on time before I got home from work."

As I pull into a parking space, the ceiling-monster dream flashes in my mind. My mouth goes dry.

"I never will forget how y'all got yourselves up for school and out the door in the morning—"

"Shut up, Mama! Just shut up!" I kill the engine. "I don't want to hear another word about how grown-up we were. Little kids should not have to get themselves up for school in the morning and put themselves to bed at night. The only reason we did was because if not, you'd beat us senseless. Are you proud of how we took *that* like a grown-up?

"And what about all the men you used to bring home? Didn't you realize we were in the same room, that we could hear you drinking your Scotch and going at each other over there in the corner? Didn't you know we were just little girls and we could hear every moan and dirty thing the men said to you? Where was our father then?"

For the first time since I can remember, tears rise to the surface and break free.

Her shaking hand flies to her mouth.

"You think you can spill all your secrets now and expect the hurt you caused to vanish? No, Mama, I don't think so."

I get out of the car because I can't bear to hear any more. As I start to walk away, I remember Summer needs help getting out and I won't leave her with Mama.

When I open Summer's door, Mama stammers, "If I could go back and do things differently, I would. Please believe me."

As Summer and I walk away with tears streaming down our faces, I feel light for the first time in my life.

The monster in the ceiling is finally dead.

CHAPTER 14

Summer

Nick calls me on my cell phone at seven o'clock the next morning.

"Did I wake you?"

"No, I just got out of the shower."

"Mmm…now there's a nice picture to start the day on."

The comment startles me at first, but then I smile. The man *had* seen me naked and at one time he knew my body better than I did. It had always been this way between us—sensual, sexy, playful.

"You letch." I weave as much sultriness into my voice as I can muster this hour of the morning.

"How's the trip so far?" he asks with a touch of wicked laughter in his voice.

I sit on the edge of the bed and towel-dry my hair. "Just peachy."

It couldn't be further from peachy, but where do I begin?

"Sounds like someone got up on the wrong side of the bed. But you never were a morning person, were you?"

"Have you ever tried to shower standing on one leg with the other one hanging over the side of the tub? Add to that I haven't had a decent cup of coffee since I left New York. Guaranteed to set your morning off on the wrong foot. Pun intended."

He chuckles and I can see him so clearly in my mind the way he used to look in the morning lying there next to me, his voice low and raspy from sleep.

I draw in a sharp breath, savoring the way he makes my belly stir. It's nice to know some things, such as the effect Nick has on me, remain constant—especially in the midst of all that had changed over night. You wake up one morning secure in the knowledge that your mother had no idea who your father was and you go to bed that night having gained a dad. It can throw a person for a loop.

"When you get back I promise to brew you one of my famous espressos."

When we were in New York, he used to wake me up with a cup of coffee on mornings that I had an early fitting.

"Promise?" I say.

"You got it. Hold on just a second. I have to take this call. I'll be right back."

I take the opportunity to pull on underwear, clean black jeans and a black sleeveless mock turtleneck. I wonder if we'll drink the espresso in bed the morning after a long sleepless night of getting reacquainted. My body aches for him for about ten seconds until I remember Jordan, the little boy who shares his house and dictates his life.

The daydream of spontaneous sex with my ex evaporates like a splash of cold water on hot pavement, replaced by the thought of a little boy who offers his prized teddy bear and his own personal boo-boo bunny to people who are hurt. I guess that comes so naturally because he feels loved. Nick's so stable his son doesn't have to cling to possessions, because he doesn't fear life as he knows it might explode without a moment's notice.

I walk over to the little coffeemaker next to the sink and put on a pot. I might as well.

When Skye and I were growing up, Ginny was a labyrinth of contradictions. One moment she was screaming at us for not going to bed on time. The next she was shaking us awake at two-thirty in the morning because she'd brought some friends home with her for a party and wanted them to meet us. Summer and I would greet them sleepily and by that time she'd have the couch folded up and the music on the stereo. Everyone was usually half-lit and dancing and carrying on until neighbors either pounded on the door or called the police.

Summer and I would curl up in the corner with our pillows and blankets, trying our best to stay out of the way.

During the happy times Ginny loved loud music and wild, drunken parties. *Fun, fun, fun! Go, go, go!* She never slept. She was superhuman, larger than life. She could spin the world on her index finger.

When the world fell, it shattered into a million tiny pieces at her feet. We were left to pick up the pieces and do our best not to get cut.

It all makes sense now. And in a way it feels better

to know Ginny had no control over her moods. We weren't the ones pushing her over the edge.

"I'm back," Nick says. "I'm sorry to put you on hold. I'm picking up some freelance work and that was the client."

"What are you doing?"

"A commercial shoot for a company that produces plastics. Not very interesting, I'm afraid, but therein lies the challenge. To make plastic appear fascinating."

"Oh, I get it. No different than a fashion shoot."

We laugh and that old familiar warmth draws out. "I found out Ginny's motive for dragging us on the road."

"Something other than finding Jane?"

I run a brush through my hair.

"Remember all those stories I told you about Ginny's younger, wilder days? How she always said she had no idea who our father was?"

"Right."

"She knew."

"You're kidding."

"I wish I were. Have you heard of a man named Robert English?"

Nick's quiet for a minute, thinking, I presume. "Former Florida Governor Robert English?" he asks.

"Or Dad, as I now call him. Well, I can if I ever meet him."

"You're joking."

"Do I sound like I'm joking?"

"Wow, Summer. I don't know what to say."

"That makes two of us. She told us last night. Skye freaked, of course. I don't know. She lied to us, Nick, all these years. I'm forty years old. I finally find out I have a father and I don't know a damn thing about him." I slump down on the foot of the bed.

"Maybe I can help with that?"

"I doubt it."

"You underestimate me, love."

Despite the way I feel, my heart does a little flutter at the endearment.

"The magic of the Internet can reveal a lot."

"You're going to do a search on him? I don't know, Nick. Maybe I don't want to know that much about him. The more you know about someone makes you want to know them that much more—or not at all, depending on the findings?"

"I'll screen it for you. Let me take a look and see what I can find."

I hear him typing in the background. I pour myself a cup of what's managed to brew—nearly half a cupful—and burn my mouth because I take a sip too soon.

Wincing, I touch the place where the coffee scalded my lip. I'm about to put some lip balm on it when there's a knock at the door. Reflexively, my shoulder muscles tense, because I fear it might be Ginny. She had the decency to not call or come knocking last night determined to hash this out. She left us in peace. Or she gave me some space at least. Maybe she went to Skye's room first and my sister bound and gagged her to force her to give it a rest.

Stranger things have happened.

I look out the peephole and breathe a sign of relief when I see Skye standing there. Pressing the phone to my ear, I open the door, let her inside and mouth, *It's Nick*.

She raises a single eyebrow and purses her lips, her trademark expression when she's in a bad humor. The dark circles under her eyes hint that she didn't sleep any better than I did.

"Hmm…here we go. Look at this," Nick says on the other end of the line.

"What is it?" I ask.

"Something I think you'll be very interested to know."

Skye and I decide to wait for Ginny in the lobby, where they serve a continental breakfast. At least I can get some coffee there. Even if it's not *good* coffee, it has to be better than the stuff they supply in the room.

On the way down to breakfast, I phone Gerard's studio. It's much too early for him to be in, but I wanted to leave a message so he could call me back at a good time for him. That always ups the chance of catching him in a good mood.

Speaking of people who aren't early risers… "Did we even tell Ginny what time to meet us? She was pretty well lit after all those drinks. I hope she found her way back to her room last night."

"I hope she has a scorching headache this morning."

I smile at my sister's ability to express what most people would only think.

"Let's eat and when we're finished if she hasn't materialized, we'll call her room."

When we walk in the front doors, the place smells of coffee and toast. Breakfast is set up in a good-size area directly across from the front desk. I didn't notice it last night when we checked in because it was closed off by a set of French doors running the length of the office.

There's a series of buffet tables in the center with packages of various breakfast cereals and oatmeal, a variety of fruits, juices and breads, doughnuts and Danishes.

About fifteen tables are arranged around the room, all of them full. I grab coffee, two packets of Equal and an apple Danish and keep a close eye on a man and woman who appear to be almost finished.

When they leave I grab it in time for Skye to return with a tray loaded with a bowl of oatmeal, a banana, toast, juice, coffee and a half pint of skim milk.

She settles herself and pours some of the milk into her oatmeal.

"Sometime around three o'clock this morning, it dawned on me that all these years, I've been harboring a lot of unresolved anger toward Mama," she says as she butters her toast. She's donning her amateur psychologist's hat. She'd be a good therapist the way she's always psychoanalyzing everyone. She majored in liberal arts in college and never had a career beyond wife and mother. But she seemed happy until now. She and Cameron got married right after she graduated. He went to law school. She had babies and kept house.

"Summer, I think we both harbor a lot of anger toward Mama."

"For obvious reasons," I say.

"I think we've been so determined to pretend that everything is perfect in our lives—you know, play the hand we've been dealt, make lemons out of the lemonade—that we've brushed the anger aside rather than dealing with it head-on."

I'm tempted to point out that she's the one who's preoccupied with perfect—the perfect house, the perfect husband, the perfect kids, the perfect upper-middle-class image that she works so hard to present to the friends who populate her perfect little world—but given her state of mind, it probably wouldn't be a good idea to tell her so.

Me? I'm terribly flawed and I'll be the first to admit it.

"I don't get it? Is acknowledging our anger supposed to make it go away?"

"It's a start. It's the first step in the healing process."

"So we say, 'Ginny, I've been really pissed at you for a long time,' and then what?"

"I don't know, Summer. I wish I did."

We sit in silence for a while. I look at the people gathered in this room—mostly families, probably heading home after a vacation or maybe just starting on the adventure. Typical families enjoying the freedom of summer vacation.

We never took vacations when Skye and I were little. I wonder for a minute what it would have been like, how our lives would have been different if we'd been a typical family. If our father would have loved our mother and chosen to make a family with her. If he'd been there for us like Nick's there for Jordan.

"When I talked to Nick this morning, he did a search on Robert English—or should we call him Daddy?"

"Summer! You told him?"

"Why not?"

"Because. I haven't even had time to digest this. I don't want the rest of the world to know."

"Don't be ridiculous. Nick's not going to blab. Didn't you call Cameron last night and tell him?"

Her lips purse, and her left eyebrow goes up. "I didn't talk to Cameron last night. Anyway, Nick's not family. This is a serious *family* matter that should be confined to *family* only."

"Oh, give me a break, Skye. He used to be my husband and he's still my friend."

"Until the day before yesterday, you hadn't talked to him in years. He's not exactly trustworthy."

Oh. Okay, I see where this is going. It has nothing to do with me *telling* Nick as much as it has to do with me *marrying* Nick. But I don't have the energy to debate that right now.

"Well, do you want to hear what he had to say or not?"

Skye doesn't answer me. She spoons oatmeal into her mouth, then dabs her lips at the corners with her napkin. Since she doesn't say no, I take it to mean yes.

"Our father still lives in Tallahassee."

Skye goes pale and sets down her plastic spoon.

"The information was right there on the first page of the search. It seems Daddy dear is a spokesperson for Majestic Oaks Retirement Community right there in Tallahassee. He was in a testimonial ad they ran in the *Tallahassee Democrat*. The retirement community uses it on their Web site. Looks like a pretty ritzy place."

Skye blinks and takes a deep breath. "To think all these years, I've lived in the same city as my father and I didn't even know it."

"I think when we get back from this road trip, we should pay our father a visit."

Skye slams her palm on the table. "Absolutely not!"

The people at the next table look at us.

"Don't you think he deserves to know he has two daughters?" I whisper.

Skye shakes her head.

"Don't you think he owes us something? At least the acknowledgment that he's our father?"

"I've lived this long without him in my life. I sure don't need him now. In fact, I see no reason why Mama's revelations should go beyond the three of us—oh and Nick, who'd better keep his mouth shut."

I lean in. "You're acting like this is fodder for a world-class scandal. Get over yourself."

Skye looks genuinely shocked. "Maybe in your arena it's not, but I live in Tallahassee. Cameron practices law in Tallahassee and hasn't completely ruled out the possibility of running for public office."

"You're not serious." I try to picture my sister as the first lady of Florida or the United States and for some quirky reason, I can see it. Skye as a modern-day Jackie Kennedy. But then all of a sudden dozens of skeletons come tumbling out of her closet.

It just won't work.

Skye makes a face and waves me off.

"Mama has achieved some local notoriety through her philanthropy and while the fact that the father of her twin babies is a rather colorful former governor and presidential candidate might not be a world-class scandal, as you put it, it could be significant if it got out."

"And what better way to make him acknowledge us after all those years of no support?"

"Do you realize how potentially damaging this could be to a lot of people? Even if it doesn't adversely affect you?"

"Don't make your life into a soap bubble that is so fragile anyone can pop it, Skye."

I can almost see her gritting her teeth. "Summer, my life is *not* a soap bubble and I don't appreciate your trivializing it. There's more at stake here than you realize. So consider others and think beyond yourself for change."

What is this? A damn universal theme? First Nick preaching about it, now my sister?

Then I look over and see Ginny walk through the doors.

CHAPTER 15

Ginny

I tossed and turned all night wondering whether my girls would leave me stranded in the middle of nowhere now that they know the truth. Then I cried myself to sleep because I wouldn't blame them if they did.

And I want to cry again this morning when I see them in the lobby downstairs, albeit distant and cold, but they're here.

I couldn't ask for more. Except maybe for my Jane to be here with me. But all in good time.

I grab a cup of coffee—I don't have the stomach for food this morning—and we get back on the road.

Moody clouds hanging in the eastern sky are pink and swollen. Looks like morning stayed out all night and was embarrassed to be caught creeping home.

I know how she feels. I didn't stay out, but I feel

as if I'm creeping home. Home to my girls after all these years.

I'm quiet and let them take the lead. I piled a lot on them yesterday. Maybe I shouldn't have done it that way, but Lord, I don't see how I could have done it any different.

I just don't see how I could have convinced them to listen to the whole thing without walking away. Maybe it seems manipulative, but in the end, I really think they'll thank me for it.

About an hour into the silent journey, Skye says, "Why did you lie to us?"

I should have been prepared. I knew it was coming, but what more can I say than what I said last night?

"Skye, darlin', there's no other reason than what I told you. I wish I had a better answer for you, baby girl, but I don't."

"Don't call me baby girl." She spits the words through gritted teeth. "Don't call me that again."

I can tell the last leg of this journey is going to be the longest part of the trip. I just hope by the time we get back to Dahlia Springs, she'll have mellowed.

"Ginny, answer one question for me," Summer

pipes up from the backseat. "What are we supposed to do with this? I can understand and even appreciate your telling us about your battle with bipolar disorder, but telling us about our father...now. Why? What are we supposed to do with that?"

"We're not supposed to do anything with it," Skye quips. "I think she simply needed to unburden herself and we were her dumping ground."

"Skye, darlin', that is not true."

She rolls her eyes. "Oh, so now the woman who lived a lie is talking about what's true."

A migraine is brewing behind my eyes, and I lean my head against the window. "How long are you going to punish me, darlin'? Because I just want to let you know that no matter how long it is, I can take it." I close my eyes against the pain. "I'll be right here when you're done."

"I say we all three go see Robert English and settle this matter with him," says Summer.

We're approaching a rest stop and Skye jerks the wheel to the right, merges onto the exit and steers the car into a parking place. She kills the engine, removes her seat belt and turns around to face her sister.

"We are going to hash this out right now and

then I don't want to hear another word about Robert English. Do you understand?"

"Oh, get over yourself." Summer leans forward and I swear for a minute there's going to be a catfight right here in this car.

"Why would you do that, Summer? What do you expect to gain by approaching him? Are you looking for a payoff? Is that what you want? An inheritance or something—"

"That's *not* what I'm after."

As much as I should stay out of this, I feel the need to intervene.

"Whether or not you decide to contact your father is up to you. I can guarantee you it's going to come as big a shock to him as it did to you. So you need to each think long and hard about it before you do that. I just beg you not to make a rash decision and I hope you'll come to a mutual agreement. Whatever that is, whatever you decide amongst the two of you, I'll support."

"We're not going to do it," says Skye. "She doesn't seem to realize that a man as connected as Robert English isn't going to welcome his illegitimate daughters waltzing into his regal world, turning it upside down. Summer, even if you simply ask him to acknowledge us, it's going to be an uphill fight that will drag everyone through the mud. So just leave it alone."

"I'm not going to leave this alone." Summer's voice goes up several decibels. "How can I? You don't want me to upset your *regal world*. You are so spoiled living on easy street, no thanks to anything you've done to earn the money, but only because you married well."

I cover my ears to block out the yelling. "Stop it! Girls, just stop fighting! Please. I swear it was not my intention to upset y'all this way. I was hoping that getting rid of all the secrets would set us on the road to a better relationship. I'm just so sick and tired of secrets."

But Skye carries on, raising her voice over mine as if she hasn't heard a word I said.

"It's that damn entitlement attitude that's gotten you where you are today. We had the same wide-open field of choices. So don't you point your finger at me accusing me of marrying well like it's a crime. You made your choice and you chose to marry Nick Russo after you stole him from me. You got exactly what you deserved. A cad who'd leave one sister for the other wasn't likely to stick around long, much less support you like a man should."

I'm about ready to get out of the car when Summer lowers her voice.

"That's what this is really about, isn't it?" Her voice is so still it's eerie. "You've never gotten over Nick marrying me. Well, I have news for you. Too many years have gone by. You have a husband and a family. You need to get over it. It was just one of those things that happened, Skye. We didn't do it to spite you or to hurt you. We fell in love and it really had nothing to do with you."

Skye rests her head against the headrest, closes her eyes for a moment. "You are so utterly clueless." She sits up again and turns to look her sister square in the eye. "I *do not* want Nick Russo. As far as I'm concerned, you two can have each other. You deserve each other. It's the principle of the matter, Summer. You betrayed me. My own sister."

Skye's voice cracks.

Summer falls back against the seat, looking like she's had all the wind knocked out of her.

"My own twin," Skye whispers. "We were supposed to be so much alike, but we never were. Everything always came easy to you. I had to work my butt off to even get noticed."

"That's not true—" says Summer.

"You know it is. The boys always preferred you." Her voice wavers and I wonder for a minute if she's going to cry. She blinks, swallows hard and says through gritted teeth, "And when a guy finally looked twice at me, you took him from me. Not only did I lose my boyfriend when you did that, I lost my sister, my friend, the only person in the world I thought I could trust."

Summer shakes her head. "Skye, you were the smart one, the brave one."

"Guys aren't interested in that. You and Mama know all about that. You all got some gene I didn't get."

A tear rolls down Summer's cheek. "What would I have done without you? All those times *she* checked out?"

She swats in my direction, and it hurts, but I need to give them time to process everything. It's obviously bringing up a lot more than I realized it would. But that's okay. This confrontation over Nick Russo has been a long time coming. It's good they're finally clearing the air.

CHAPTER 16

Skye

We drive for miles in silence. Over narrow, rolling two-lane highways and tree-lined Ozark Mountain roads. I stare straight ahead down the road as if looking hard enough, I'll see the light on the other side of all the issues between us.

We are a screwed-up lot. I wonder how we're going to help Jane when the three of us can't even help ourselves?

Emptiness engulfs me and I wonder about the toll this trip is going to take on the shanty of a relationship we had before we started on this journey.

It's a wonder we're all three still in the same car, but we are. Mama's got her jacket rolled up into a pillow, her head resting against the window. I can't see Summer in the rearview mirror, but at least she's stopped going on about contacting Robert English.

The sound of the car engine draws out my thoughts and entices me to mull over all that's unfolded in the past twenty-four hours.

I wonder how Cameron will take the news of my father?

Actually, I know how he'll take the news. Not well. Reflexively, I glance at my phone. It's in its place plugged into the charger. He hasn't called back.

Cameron, what's happening to us? What's going to become of us once the kids are grown and we don't have them to hide behind anymore?

I was a virgin on my wedding night.

I always thought I was saving myself for the man I loved. It was such a precious part of me to give to a man, I didn't want to throw it away on just anyone.

I suppose Mama's antics had something to do with me waiting. I didn't want it to be like that. I wanted…love.

When I met Cameron and he was willing to wait, I knew I'd found someone special.

It was difficult developing lasting relationships in college. Most boys were out for one thing and one thing only, and when I wouldn't give it to them it was on to the next. I always wondered if Nick dumped me for Summer because I wouldn't put out?

Not that I know the intimacies of their relationship—Summer and I don't discuss things like that—but a man doesn't live with a woman for ten years before they get married if he's not getting a little *somethin'-somethin'*. In the beginning, I didn't want to hear about her escapades with Nick. Now, given the state of my marriage and that she's alone, I wonder if either of us would even have anything to report?

It's a topic better left untouched. Because I suspect our opinions on sex differ greatly. I don't think sex is all it's cracked up to be—at least that's what I've always thought. It shouldn't be the foundation of a relationship. Because if you don't have more than that, when you hit the dry spells, what do you have left?

Cameron and I have been in a dry spell for about five years. I mean we still have sex, but if we're together once a month, that's a lot. I just don't have the drive I used to—I've gained weight and that doesn't exactly make one feel sexy, especially when you go into Victoria's Secret and end up looking like the big top at the circus rather than the model on the front of the catalogue.

It doesn't do a whole lot for a woman's self-image. If the foundation of our relationship wasn't built on something a whole lot firmer, I might be worried.

My sister and I really don't have that much in common other than our blood ties. I always felt a little cheated—like a phony, having a twin and being so un-twinlike. Like maybe my soul slipped into the wrong body when we were born.

I wonder if she and Nick are going to reconcile, since they've been talking lately? I wouldn't begrudge them. I said my bit and I will get beyond it.

Maybe it goes back to all that unresolved anger I was talking about before. Maybe the question is, once you acknowledge anger, does it fade away?

When we pass a sign that says we're eighty miles outside of Springvale, Ginny stretches.

"We're getting close now," she says at the end of a yawn. "How you doing, sweetie? Need me to drive?"

"No, Mama, thank you. I'm fine."

I hear Summer stir, too.

"Does anyone need to stop for a break?"

"I sure could use a potty and a stretch," says Mama.

I take the first exit and pull into a Burger King in Cabool, Missouri. Mama offers to help Summer out of the backseat, but my sister declines. "I need to talk to Skye for a minute."

Mama gets out and goes into the restaurant by herself. I hesitate because I'm weary. I'm tired of fighting and I don't think I can go one more round with her over Robert English or Nick or—

"Skye, I am so sorry for hurting you."

Her voice trembles on the last word. I almost ask her to repeat it, because I'm not sure I heard her right. But then it sinks in. I wave her off, pretending it's not an issue anymore.

"I said my piece. I'm over it." I suddenly feel claustrophobic, like I need to get out of the car. I reach for the door handle, but I don't open it. A little cavern of hope opens up inside me. I swallow against it, filling it up with all the reasons I shouldn't hope. Too much baggage, too much hurt, too much pain.

Too much. Too much. Too much.

"Do you have any idea how I looked up to you when we were growing up—how I depended on you?"

"I'm not sure if that's a good thing."

"You were always so perfect—"

"Nobody's perfect."

"Everything you did—straight As. Always picking up the slack when Ginny dropped the ball, which was more often than not. You went to college...."

"And you can see what I'm doing with it."

"Skye, where's the confidence you used to have when we were young? You could march right into the fire and come out the other side."

I shake my head and I feel the chasm inside me widen, ready to expose all my faults and fears and ugly imperfections.

"I don't know what would have happened to us if you hadn't been there. I certainly couldn't have handled it the way you did. I am truly sorry for hurting you. Like Ginny says, if I could go back and undo it, I would."

Then right there in the Burger King parking lot, she does something that floors me. She leans forward and hugs me. Really hugs me, like I can't remember her ever doing before.

Ginny

I buy lunch for us to give the girls more time to talk. As I stand in line, I try to see through the store window, but the sun is reflecting off the glass, obscuring my vision. These old eyes aren't as good as they used to be, anyway.

All I can do is hope the girls are out there making their peace with each other.

The line's moving slow. I'm eager to get back on the road. Eager to get to my baby girl. It sends a shiver through my body when I think that I'll probably be seeing her in just under three hours. I wonder how she's doing. If she's healthy or hungry. When was the last time she had a decent meal? I thank God it's warm outside so she's not cold at night.

Oh, Jane, how are you going to react when you see us? I utter a silent prayer that she'll come home with us without a fuss.

I get the order to go and carry the food outside. When I get in the car, Skye's turned around talking to Summer. The air feels lighter. Like they've worked something out. But I don't ask. If they want to tell me, they will.

We eat our lunch in the parking lot and get back on the road. We're all tired of traveling, and I suspect the girls are eager to get this trip over with. I think we're all a little anxious over seeing Jane. Not the good kind of anxious. The kind that knots your stomach and leaves you hoping for the best.

CHAPTER 17

Summary

When we arrive in Springvale, Ginny directs Skye to the women's shelter in the old Indigo Hotel on Commercial Street.

"It looks exactly as it did all those years ago, just a little worn with age. Back in the twenties this used to be the place to stay. But you'd never know by looking at it now."

I squint and try to see it through Ginny's eyes. I guess if you look beyond the dust and the peeling paint you can see the bones of grandeur.

We park on the street in front of the building and make our way to the director's office. The sign on the open office door says Laura Kane.

I knock and a slim woman with dark hair looks up from her paperwork and smiles. "May I help you?"

"We're hoping Jane Hamby is here?"

The woman shakes her head. "She's out right now. Is there something I can help with?"

"Darlin', I wish you could," says Ginny.

Laura Kane looks at her watch. "If you hurry, you might be able to find her on the corner of Commercial Street and Boonville down at the square."

Laura Kane points out toward the front of the shelter. "Did you park out front?"

I nod.

"That's Commercial Street. Just follow it until it dead-ends at Boonville."

We thank her and pile back into the car.

When we get to the square, we see her. Small and skinny, wearing threadbare clothing and holding up a tattered sign that simply asks, "Why?"

We watch Jane from the car for a few minutes. Seeing her standing there in her tattered jeans and T-shirt worn so thin you can see through it in places breaks my heart. When she takes a step toward a person who is approaching, I can see that her shoe has a hole in the bottom of it.

None of us speak. My heart is heavy. As people

pass she hands them a piece of paper. Some even stop and put money in a cigar box at her feet.

Ginny sobs. "How could I have let this happen?"

I scoot forward on the seat and put a hand on my mother's shoulder. "I think we all feel that way. But how do you help a person who doesn't want to be helped?"

I meant the words to comfort, but Ginny sobs. "Oh, just look at her. I should have made more of an effort to find her earlier."

"Mama, she didn't want to be found. That's why she moved around all the time. We just have to accept that this is how she wanted things. She's skinny, but she looks relatively well."

Ginny nods, but the nod slowly changes direction and she's shaking her head.

"We just have to accept that and move forward from here. Finding my sweet Jane is like discovering the missing piece of a puzzle that's been incomplete for far too long."

I watch Ginny looking around the square. I wonder if the places are familiar and hold significance, or if time and distance have made them vague and foreign?

Does this place feel like an albatross or a curse, maybe?

But then again, she's always been a firm believer in making your own luck. I mean, look at how far she's come. She's living proof that if you let something drag you down it's your own fault.

You've just gotta pick yourself up and trudge on ahead.

We wait until Jane finishes talking to a man who's dropped a bill into the cigar box. Then we get out of the car and approach her.

She just stands there gripping her sign, staring straight at us as if trying to place our faces. No one speaks for what seems an eternity.

"Jane?" Ginny finally breaks the silence. "Baby?"

"Oh my God." Jane throws down the sign and papers and runs, leaving the cigar box on the sidewalk.

"Jane!" Ginny sinks to her knees and buries her face in her hands, sobbing.

About fifteen yards away Jane stops. She stands with her back to us for a few beats and then turns.

"What the hell do you want?"

CHAPTER 18

Summer

"We just want to make sure you're okay," Ginny pleads through her tears. "Baby, please don't run away from us."

Skye and I take Ginny by the arm and help her get to her feet. Jane throws up her hands and mutters something to the heavens, but she walks back to us.

She points a finger at Skye. "I can't believe you brought them here. I should have never trusted you."

Skye points a finger at Jane. "Now you wait just a minute. Is this what I get for helping you? You are a *spoiled brat*."

Ginny and I look at Skye.

"What are you talking about?" I ask.

Jane heaves an exasperated sigh and turns to walk away again.

"Why is it always about you, Jane?" says Skye. "Why can't you stop for a change and see how you're hurting everyone else? Mama bent over backwards giving you a good life to make up for some imagined karmic debt she thought she owed for being such a bad mother to *us*. To *us*. And we drive halfway across the country for you to give us the middle finger because you think you've had it so bad?"

"Nobody asked you to come."

"Nobody said we wanted to come," she says. "We're here because Mama and Summer wanted to make sure you were okay."

"You could have just told them I was fine."

"They didn't know I knew until you opened your big mouth."

I'm stunned. I can't believe Skye knew where Jane was all along and didn't tell us or at least tell Ginny—

"You knew?" I murmur.

But Skye doesn't hear me. "Mama almost died. How would you have felt if you'd never seen her again?"

"She knew?" I repeat.

Jane's mouth falls open like she wants to say something, but she just stands there in shocked silence.

In the midst of everything, Ginny holds up her hands and says, "I don't care who knew what. Jane, we came because even if it's just for one brief moment, I wanted my family together. I love you all and I just needed this no matter how short a time it is."

I see a visible change wash over Jane as she stands there gaping first at Ginny, then at Skye and me.

"Will you at least let me take you to get some dinner?" Ginny asks.

Jane bites her bottom lip and nods. "Sure, Mom, that would be nice. But first I have to take the money back to the shelter."

"Can't you just leave it in the car? We can put it in the console and I'll lock up. No one will steal it. In fact, it'll probably be safer there than at the shelter."

"Nope. It's policy. I can't have the money out overnight. I have to put it in the safe and the office closes at five. I don't want to lose my job over it."

"Job?" The three of us say the word in unison.

Jane looks at us. It's a total Ginny expression. At that moment, she looks just like her.

"I work at the Indigo." Her voice is laced with annoyance, as if she's ready to defend herself. So tough for one so petite.

We must be looking as if we don't understand because she says, "The Indigo Hotel. The women's shelter. I'm training to be the assistant director."

"You *work* there?" Skye asks.

"I thought you were the one who'd been keeping up with her," I say.

"I had no idea she was working there. I thought she was staying there."

"Don't talk about me like I'm not here. I used to stay there, but now I work there. Is that a problem?"

Ginny beams. "I am so proud."

Ever the killjoy, I say, "If you work there, what's with the sign?"

"I stand in the square an hour a day passing out leaflets because the government is making noises about cutting the shelter's funding."

Oh. We all make relieved noises, understanding what she's saying.

"I have to admit when I saw you holding the Why? sign, I thought you were homeless. I thought it was a new spin on the *will work for food* gig," says Skye. "Rather than a false promise it's a philosophical question."

Jane obviously misses the humor in Skye's thought.

"I *did* live in the shelter. Months ago, in fact. The people there—and Skye's care packages and support—saved my life." She says it solemnly as if challenging any one of us to question her.

We take Jane back to the Indigo so she can turn in the money. She gives us a quick tour of the place and we go to a little Italian restaurant for dinner. The place has red-and-white-checkered tablecloths, Chianti bottles as candleholders and delicious northern Italian food.

Picking at her antipasto, Ginny says, "Baby, why didn't you just come home or at least get in touch with me?"

Jane gazes at her, as if weighing her words. I want to tell Jane *I* understand. I know how Ginny can be—overbearing and demanding. Her way or the highway. It's not as easy as *just coming home*.

I understand that, Jane.

She closes her eyes for a moment. Opens them. "I've been on medication. But I've really only been stable for a couple of months. It was too soon, Mom. Plus, I suppose a part of me needed to stand on my own two feet—find my own way—before I could find my way home."

Hear, hear, little sister.

Ginny reaches across the table and takes Jane's hand in both of hers. "You're doing so well, baby."

Jane ducks her head. Long lashes obscure her eyes.

"I thought I'd messed up so badly, Mom, you wouldn't want me back."

"Nonsense, angel! I love you, your sisters love you. No matter what, you always have a home with me. All three of my girls will always have a place in my home. In fact, Jane, why don't you let us take you back with us?"

Jane smiles and shakes her head. "I have finally found my place in the world." Her eyes shine. "Working at the shelter is my calling. It saved my life. Now I want to give back and help someone else."

Her streetwise guard is down and, despite her unkempt hair and threadbare clothes, she looks beautiful and young and full of promise.

I feel bad for doubting her, but I also could never forgive myself if I'd sent money to finance a drug habit. It was a crap shoot, not unlike life. I chose wrong.

"Jane, you must think I'm pretty callous to have cut you off the way I did, especially since *some-*

one—" I give Skye a pointed look "—never bothered
to tell us she was still sending money."

Ginny snorts. "I didn't know either of you were
still in touch with her after she cut ties with me."
Ginny's voice is light, but there's a note of truth in
her words. "If anyone has a right to be angry, it's me."

Jane stares at her hands, flexes her fingers, then
squeezes them together in a nervous fidget. "Summer,
remember how you begged me to come live with you
until I got back on my feet? How could I ever think you
were callous? But I couldn't live with you. I wasn't *there*
yet. You know what I'm saying? But I'm okay now."

Ginny's a little quiet, sitting there just taking it all
in. Skye reaches across the table and squeezes Ginny's
hand. "I guess we've all had our secrets, Mama."

Ginny nods and a tear meanders down her cheek.
She squeezes Skye's hand back. "It's okay, baby.
It's okay."

Ginny

We drive my sweet Jane home after dinner. She
shows off her little apartment in a quadruplex about
two-thirds of a mile from the Indigo.

It's a small one-bedroom with a window-unit air conditioner/heater and modest furnishings: couch, coffee table, end table and chair in the living room. Full-size bed and dresser in the bedroom. There's barely enough room to turn around in the kitchen, and it's not in the best part of town, but there's a good dead bolt on the door and the place is clean and safe.

She says it's part of the shelter's transitional housing program. Once she's saved enough money she'll be able to move out and get a place of her own.

There's no telephone, but at least I know my baby isn't sleeping on the street at night. She can come in and lock her door, have a nice hot bath, fix herself a meal and rest her head on a pillow.

I excuse myself to go to the bathroom, which is located off the bedroom, and while I'm there, I pull five one-hundred-dollar bills out of my wallet and tuck them in her underwear drawer. As I rejoin the others, I take in the place my baby girl calls home— the neatly made bed, how there are no dirty dishes in the sink. She doesn't have much, but everything's in its place.

She had no idea she was havin' company tonight. Yet, look at this place. Neat as a pin.

It makes me smile.

CHAPTER 19

Skye

W e leave the next day after Mama argues with Jane about a cell phone. Mama wants to go get her one so they can talk. Jane doesn't want one because, she says, they're a nuisance.

"You can call me at work if you need me. Here's my business card."

Jane wins.

Mama's so proud to get the card that you would've thought it was made of platinum.

We promise to keep in touch, wave goodbye to Jane and set off for home.

After we've been on the road about an hour, Mama says, "Thank God in heaven for that place. Who knows what would have happened to Jane if not for them? They are going on the foundation's permanent list of recipients." She takes a small leather-bound notebook from her purse and writes a note to herself.

"You know, Ginny, why not start an organization that helps women get back on their feet?"

"I'm listening," she says. "What kind of organization would it be?"

"That's a good question." In the rearview mirror, I see Summer gaze out the window for a moment. "When Jane gave us the tour of the Indigo, she mentioned that one of the biggest misconceptions about the homeless is that they're lazy, that they'd rather loiter than work. But how do you get a job when you don't have a place to wash up, or clean clothes to wear to the interview, much less a contact address and telephone number? Going into the interview, the deck is already stacked against them. She said she was lucky because she found her job within the shelter, but one of the biggest boosts a homeless person can get is a decent outfit to wear when they interview. It doesn't have to be fancy, just clean and in good repair. Once a person gets a job it makes them feel like a worthwhile, contributing human being, which sets the spiral turning upward."

"*Hmm,*" says Ginny. "That's interesting. It's truly not just a handout. It's a leg up."

"The Junior League chapter I belong to operates a thrift store, but most of the items in there seem brand-new. I wonder if we could somehow partner with them or at least model it after their concept?"

Ginny makes more notes in her little book. "Sounds like you all are going to have this organization planned by the time we get home. The foundation would love to fund such a worthwhile venture, but who's going to run it?"

Summer and I make noncommittal noises and the conversation fades into silence.

Is it any wonder? Our worlds have been turned upside down on this trip and we are returning different people than we started out.

It's life altering to learn the mother you thought was a commune-dwelling free spirit was actually a troubled soul plagued by mental illness—that she kept these secrets bottled up all these years because she thought it would do more harm than good if she laid the goods on the table.

But it also feels good to be free of secrets.

Later, as Summer snoozes in the backseat with her

broken foot stretched out in front of her, I say, "Mama, I feel I owe you an explanation. I never told you I knew where Jane was because I—"

Mama touches my arm. "Baby, you don't have to explain. We've all had our secrets. If there's one thing I've learned—it's that the only way we can live fully and love unconditionally is if we all forgive each other and let go of idealized notions. Nobody's perfect. Just promise me that from this day forward we will accept each other as we are— foibles and all."

"At first, I was really miffed that you'd continued to send Jane money when we agreed not to," Summer pipes up from the backseat. "But after spending time with Jane, I realize it was probably the distance that you put between yourself and Jane that made the arrangement work. You trusted her to do the right thing with the money you sent, Skye. I put too much pressure on Jane to be accountable, to con-form to my standards when Jane wasn't in a place to do it.

"It just may have been your trust that saved her life."

I glance in the rearview mirror. Summer looks

thoughtful, then she says, "I have a suggestion for the name of the organization. How 'bout Three Sisters?"

CHAPTER 20

Summer

Crossing the Florida state line feels like re-entering the earth's atmosphere after floating in outer space—or some alternate universe—for the past four days.

I've had a tune that I can't place stuck in my head since we left on this trip and suddenly it dawns on me that it's the song Jordan was humming the night we went to the Dairy Queen.

I give myself a mental shake and try to replace it with another tune, but it keeps superimposing itself over the song.

God, I need to get back to work or do something other than sit around humming kids' songs to myself. That reminds me I have no idea what I'm doing— how I'm going to navigate the six flights of steps up to my apartment (it's a walk-up) and that Gerard never returned my call from two days ago. I hope he got the message. Why wouldn't he? The receptionist, Alma, is good about giving him his messages. It would cost her job if she wasn't.

I decide to call again, to check in and see what he's decided he wants to do with me while I'm incapacitated. A little twist of excitement forms in my belly and as I listen to the ring on the other end of the line, I gaze at my boot-clad foot and think that sometimes things happen for a reason. Maybe I would have gone on years letting him fit the clothes to me rather than taking a leap of faith into something I'd always wanted to do—like trying my hand at design. There's a big difference between modeling and designing—beyond the obvious. As a house model all I have to do to stay at the top of my game is stay slim, practice good hygiene (although that's optional at some studios) and stay free of broken bones; designing is more…personal. It's as if they're rejecting you when they pan your creations or loving you when they love your work.

I suppose that's why I haven't pushed too hard up to now. I kept thinking I wasn't ready. But now it's as if the universe has driven me up to the edge of the cliff and is saying if you don't take the leap of faith, I'm going to push you over.

"Geandeau," sings a sweet voice.

"Hello, Alma. It's Summer, again. May I speak to Gerard?"

"Oh, Summer!" Her voice is as bright as the runway spotlights. "How's the foot?"

"It'll be fine. It just takes time to heal."

"You hang in there. We miss you. When will you be back?"

"That's what I want to talk to Gerard about. I can't do a lot of standing, but I want to get back to work."

"Did he call you back?"

"No."

"I told him to call you." She sighs. "He's been incorrigible lately. Let me get him. Hold on a sec."

Ginny and Skye are chatting in the front seat. Suddenly, I'm glad we made this trip…it's been good for all of us. Yes, good all the way around.

"Geandeau." The French male voice on the other end of the line is brusque.

"Hi, Gerard. It's Summer. How are you?"

"Busy."

There's a long pause. I give him room to go off on one of his famous harangues about *this one* or *another* doing *this* or *that* and it's *really* pissed him off—

"What do you need?" That's all he says and there's a chill to his voice that freezes out Alma's warmth.

"I'd like to talk to you about what I'm going to be doing when I come back to work."

He yells something in French.

"Excuse me—?"

His French tirade collides with my question and I realize he's not even talking to me. He screams in French for a full three minutes and I wonder if I should hang up. He's obviously in one of his moods. I'm afraid that if I did hang up it would make the situation worse when I called back. So I hold until he finally says, "Goddammed imbecile."

I hope he's not talking to me. "Pardon?"

"Not you." Then, "What did you want?"

Don't take it personally. He's stressed. He always gets like this in the middle of the collections—

"Oh, right, what am I going to with you?" More yelling, at least this time it sounds as if he's put his hand over the receiver.

"I don't have time to deal with you right now."

Deal with me? As in dealing with a problem or handling a temperamental individual? If it were the latter, he wouldn't say that aloud to the person who needed to be handled. My mouth goes dry.

"Come to the studio this evening at eleven-thirty. I should be able to make some time for you then."

"Gerard, I'm sorry, I can't do that. I'm still in Florida."

More French yelling. My stomach knots because this time I have a feeling it might be directed at me.

"Well, that's your problem," he says. "I'm too busy to deal with your problems because I have too many of my own. Come and see me after your foot heals, but don't bother me right now. I don't have time for this."

The line goes dead and my entire body goes numb.

"You're kidding me? You have *got* to be kidding me." I glance from the phone in my hand to the boot on my foot to Ginny's face now turned and looking at me.

"What's wrong, darlin'?"

It takes a moment before I'm able to speak. "I think I just lost my job."

"What happened?" Ginny looks as shocked as I feel. Skye adjusts the rearview mirror so she's looking at me.

I try to shake off the hurt. But it's difficult after all these years. "I think I just caught Gerard at a bad moment. I'm sure he'll call me back."

When we pull into Ginny's driveway four hours later, Gerard hasn't phoned me back. I set my mind that he'll call me at eleven-thirty when he wanted me to come in and meet with him, but the realist in me knows it's not going to happen. Still, I carry my phone with me as if I'm waiting for a call to inform me I won the Nobel Peace Prize for being willing to go back after he treated me this way. Or maybe it's more like waiting for a death row pardon.

I go sit out on the deck overlooking the ocean while I'm waiting for Nick and Jordan to come over.

I've seen Gerard unleash his cold, careless temper on others over the years. I've seen him toss assistants out onto the curb—literally—and I've seen hysterical models evicted from his studio because they were too fat or their waist too short or their breasts too large.

God, he really is a cruel, cruel, shallow man,

around whom people tiptoe, hoping not to be the next target of his anger.

Like the others, I walked the tightrope, did my best not to fall into the pit of his fury. I'd endured his tantrums, being poked with pins (sometimes on purpose, I suspected), and being the subject of his mean, offhanded personal attacks. "Will someone *please* tell Summer to lay off the bonbons? She's got lard on her ass." I hadn't eaten a *bonbon* since I moved to New York. After his berating, I invested in another full-length mirror and took care to work out even harder if my ass even looked like it might be thinking of harboring lard. But over the course of seventeen years, I thought I'd developed tenure or at least earned the right to a modicum of respect or understanding when my mother was in the hospital or I'd inadvertently broken a bone. God, I can hear him now, "Clumsy cow."

It's high tide and from my vantage point I can see all the treasures from the sea that the water washes ashore. Then I have an idea.

I go inside and get my sketch pad. I sit on the foot of the bed and sketch out a logo for Three Sisters.

Three starfish.

One for Jane in Springvale.
One for Skye in Tallahassee.
One for me in…
Where?

Skye

When I answer the door at Mama's house, the last person I expect to see is Nick Russo standing there with his little boy.

Hard to believe the last time I saw him all those years ago, I thought we were dating. Twenty-some-odd years later, here he stands, my sister's ex-husband.

I take a deep breath and paste on a smile.

Okay, I can do this. And actually it surprises me because it's not as hard as I thought it would be.

"Well, Nick Russo, come on in."

"Hi, Skye. Did you have a good trip?"

There's an awkward moment where I think neither of us knows whether we should hug or shake hands. So I step forward and hug him.

I'm glad I did because I feel nothing.

Absolutely nothing.

No pain or jealousy or anger at him for having fallen in love with my sister and not me.

It was all between Summer and me. And now I can let it go.

"We had a wonderful trip. Quite enlightening, I must say. Who's this handsome fellow?"

He beams down at the boy, and I have to admit he's probably even better looking now than he was back then, but he's not my type. No, he's for Summer through and through.

"This is my son, Jordan."

I bend down and shake his little hand. "Hi, Jordan. I'm Mrs. Woods, your daddy's old friend."

"Daddy, she kind of looks like Summer."

My breath catches and a happy buzz hums in my veins. "We're sisters. That's why we look alike. Actually, we're twins."

"Is this a house or a castle?" he asks.

"I think it's both. Why don't you go on in and have a look around and decide for yourself?"

I glance back at Nick and a certain light of understanding passes between us. As Jordan wanders off into the next room, I say, "One of the things I learned on the trip is that sister of mine still loves you. Don't let her get away this time. She's out on the deck. Go get her."

After Nick disappears into the other room, I go upstairs to call Cameron. This trip has shaken a lot of things loose in our relationship, too. It's time for some major household repairs.

CHAPTER 21

Ginny

Before Skye leaves to drive back to Tallahassee, my girls show me the logo Summer designed for Three Sisters and present me with the bones of a business plan. I squeal with delight.

They want to do this. They *really* want to do this. To make it happen. Skye wants to start a branch in Tallahassee—

"We'll have to talk to Jane," says Skye. "But I can't see why she wouldn't want to start an arm in Springvale and incorporate it into the Indigo as a service for their clients."

The only thing that's a little nebulous is Summer's not sure whether she wants to take it back to New York or—and I still can't believe she's even considering this—start the Dahlia Springs division. I suspect that may have to do with a conversation she and Nick had when he came over, but she didn't tell me the details, only said she had a lot of thinking to do.

I know where I want her, but I am willing to keep my mouth shut and not push too hard for her to move back here. It makes sense. The cost of doing business would be a lot less—

Oh, there I go again.

I have to learn to keep my big mouth shut. Summer got so mad at me after she gave Nick's boy that little tom-tom and I told him the tale of the wishing drum.

He sat down right there, his little legs curled back under him and beat on that drum for an hour. I can't imagine all the things he was wishing for.

After they left, Summer jumped all over me saying, "He's vulnerable, Mother. You don't tell a little kid that all his wishes will come true when you have no control over that. He's had too much disappointment losing his mother."

I don't even think she realized she called me *Mother*. She was a preteen the last time she called me that. And I probably shouldn't have said it, but I couldn't help myself. "If that little boy wished for a mother, you have every opportunity to make that wish come true because it's plain as day that his father is still crazy in love with you."

She stormed out of the room—well, as much as anyone on crutches could storm—muttering, "This is why I can't move back here."

But something tells me she'll come around. I don't think Nick is going to let her get away again that easily.

Land's sakes, my head is spinning with all that's happened. If Summer decides she wants to take the Three Sisters back up to New York, I'll support her decision because from the moment my girls started talking about it on the way back from Jane, I knew it was a worthwhile venture. One I'd give my eye-teeth for my girls to run.

Honestly, I feel I've been given a gift from heaven; my three girls—happy, healthy, home for the first time in their hearts.

Summer

After Skye leaves for Tallahassee, I debate whether to call Robert English and try to arrange a meeting or just show up. I finally come to the conclusion that it would be best to take my chances and drive to the Majestic Oaks Retirement Community in Tallahassee to try and meet with him face-to-face.

It's a long shot—he might be out of town or refuse to see me—but I figured I'd have a better shot of talking to him in person than over the phone. Any unscrupulous crackpot fraud could pick up the phone and dial. Since he's a former dignitary, many probably already have.

Showing up in person conveys much more sincerity since he can have me thrown out—or arrested—if he thinks I'm there to harm him.

Nick arranges for Tammy to care for Jordan overnight and the next day, he drives me to Tallahassee. If nothing else, it gives us the opportunity to be alone for a while. Maybe being with him will help me sort out what to do.

I didn't talk to Skye about visiting Robert. She was so adamantly against it while we were on the road and we left things on such a good note, I don't want to upset matters.

As a compromise, I decide my approach with English will be that I'm the daughter of his *old friend*, Ginny Galloway. See if that gets me in the door. If so, see if the association rings any bells. I won't bring up the subject of paternity, but that's not saying I won't talk about it if he does.

Right. What are the odds of that?

Bottom line, I don't want anything from him. I'm not seeking financial rewards—if I need money, I know I can turn to Ginny. I just have to satisfy my curiosity, see this man who is my father.

I invited Ginny to come, but she refused. "Robert English is a closed chapter in my book. This is something you need to do on your own. I wish your sister was going with you."

As the car hums along the highway, I turn and gaze at this man I still love, who professed last night that he still loves me and would like to try again.

He's a package deal now. Nick and the boy.

"Of course I'm looking for a mother for my child," Nick said last night. "He's first in every decision I make. Right now, I'm not asking you to move in with us and be his mother. I'm asking you to stay long enough to see if we can make it work. Because I do still love you. I suppose on a very deep level, I've never stopped."

Would it be fair to the little boy for me to barge into their life?

We arrive in Tallahassee before noon and check into the hotel.

One room.

One king-size bed.

Two people who have a lot of pent-up feelings they need to explore on a level that words won't do.

With his lips on mine and his hands on my body in places that have longed for his touch, I feel so full of love that I wonder if just maybe I have enough love for a family of three.

Later that afternoon, Nick drops me off at the Majestic Oaks Retirement Community. It's a sprawling, gated campus nestled under a canopy of trees off a meandering road.

I'm nervous by the time I find the administration building and words want to stick in my throat when I ask the cheerful woman at the desk if it's possible to see Robert English.

"I can ring his apartment. Who may I say is calling?"

"I'm the daughter of an old friend."

Fifteen minutes later a tall, stooped man with a craggy face and a shock of white hair ambles into the lobby on a walker. *My father.* And for a split second

I want to cry. Then he smiles at me the way most older men smile at young, attractive women, which makes me a little uncomfortable.

"Who is this old friend?" he asks, staring into my eyes with such startling intensity I wonder if he sees a resemblance. But I know that's just wishful thinking.

"Ginny Galloway," I say. "She used to work—"

"Yes, I remember Virginia quite well. Is she with you?"

He straightens and glances around eagerly. For an instant, I can almost see the dashing older man who stole Ginny's heart.

"No, she didn't come."

I think I see a flash of disappointment in his eyes. "Come into the dining room. Have some tea with me."

The large room is virtually empty except for the two of us and the waitstaff who seem to be readying the place for dinner. It's furnished with expensive-looking antiques and Oriental rugs. Not at all what I envisioned as a retirement community's communal dining room. He pulls out a chair for me at a table for two next to the window.

As we wait for the server to bring us our tea, he tells

me a little bit about Majestic Oaks. He's been here for about three years and they keep him on his toes.

"It's not your typical old folks home." He chuckles and gazes at me over the top of his teacup as he blows on the hot liquid. "It's a good place for an old widower like me. They keep you so busy you don't have time to get lonely."

"Do your children come visit often?" The words spill out of my mouth before I can stop them, and I hold my breath wondering where my blurt will lead.

He braces his elbows on the table. "Nope, I've outlived my only boy. He never did give me any grandchildren."

Skye's kids flash in my head and I want so badly to say, Oh, but you do have grandchildren. Three beautiful, smart kids who would knock your socks off. I'm sad to think this man who almost ran the country is all alone in the world.

The easy flow of our conversation quells my fear that he'd ask me to explain the purpose of my visit beyond the thin veil that I'm his old friend's daughter. He begins to reminisce about her.

"I've read about Ginny's philanthropic work. Sounds like she's come a long way since her days at

Florida State. Especially seeing she has a beautiful grown daughter."

"I have a twin who lives right here in Tallahassee." He searches my face for a few moments, his sad eyes gently sweeping over my features.

"Your mother and I shared a *special* relationship. I don't know what she's told you…."

My breath catches and my heart pounds in my chest. Not a panic attack. Please. I fear this might be the turning point—where he builds his case against me, denies everything. I decide I'm not going to give him the chance to push me away. Just as the panic starts to flow, his eyes take on a soft, faraway light.

"A life in politics is a rat race," he murmurs, shakes his head. "I could tell you some stories that would curl your hair. Who holds the real power behind the public persona. It's not always who you think it is. My life was not my own when I was governor and it was even worse when I was seeking the presidency.

"By the time I retired from politics after my bid for the White House, I was a jaded and disillusioned old man."

He shakes his head and takes a slow sip of tea.

"If I could go back, I'd do many things different-ly." He sets down the cup, and the saucer rattles. "What would you do differently, Summer Russo, if you could go back and change things?"

His question startles me, but I know exactly what I'd do. "I'd wouldn't have spent so much time dwelling on what *might have been* and I wouldn't have given my fears such power."

He nods and smiles a sad smile, his watery blue-green eyes the same blue-green as mine and Skye's.

"If only things in my life had been different when I met Ginny." All he does is touch my hand for one brief moment.

In that instant, I know that he knows I'm his daughter. I don't have to say anything.

He knows.

"I like your style. I'd love to meet your sister."

I call Skye.

"Hi, Nick and I are in town. There was some business that needed to be taken care of and we came to Tallahassee."

"Do you want to stay with us?" she offers.

"No, we've got a hotel, but he's doing his thing. I'm wondering if you'll meet me for coffee?"

* * *

Robert drives us to a Panera near Capital Circle. When Skye walks in and realizes who's with me, she almost bolts.

"Please, don't go," he says. "I'm the one who convinced your sister to set up this meeting. I just wanted to see you. That's all. No...pressure."

This breaks the ice and, slowly, Skye begins to thaw.

I came here seeking answers. By the end of my visit with Robert English, I found so much more: genuine peace of mind and heart.

Skye

Left to my own devices, I would've never gone to visit our father, but that headstrong Summer just couldn't leave it alone.

I've never been so grateful that my sister and I are so different. Or perhaps that my sister knew me better than I ever imagined possible.

Meeting our father will not erase the bad years, but it's helped me realize how precious family is.

The kids hung a Welcome Home banner for me in the living room.

I cried when I saw it.

Cameron wasn't mad, as I'd feared. He said he wanted to give me some room to breathe, and it didn't hurt that he was truly bogged down with a court case. I suppose our different ways of showing emotion is a *Mars-Venus* thing. But after this time apart we both agreed that we need to work on us, start planning for life after the kids grow up and leave the house.

He was all for my new venture. I'm smart enough to know that he was probably breathing a sigh of relief—"Thank God she's finally found a hobby that will get her off my back." Well, he didn't actually say that.

Really, this feels like more than a hobby or a volunteer position to fill my days. It feels like a purpose.

After all, isn't that what it's all about? Finding purpose and living up to it? Knowing people love you with or without purpose?

I think we all—Mama, Summer, Jane and I—found purpose on that trip. I think we all returned whole or at least with emotional nutrients we need to get there. With a little bit of work on all parts we can truly be a family—all of us—for the first time in our lives.

Summer

The next day as Nick and I drive back to Dahlia Springs, I don't believe I've ever seen the sun quite so bright, the sky so blue. I feel like a sea of contradictions—on one level, I feel weightless and fulfilled, but when it comes to Nick my longing is anything but satisfied.

I suppose I need a break from the city. If I'm going to start a new life, Dahlia Springs is as good a place as any.

All these emotions merge into one beautiful feeling as I am filled with insane joy and thankfulness and awe over what has happened to me—to us.

I remind myself to tell Ginny that maybe it *is* possible to go home again.

EPILOGUE

Five years later Robert English dies. He recognizes Ginny Galloway and his daughters, Skye Woods and Summer Russo, in his last will and testament.

Just let it shine, it's payback time!

When a surprise inheritance brings
an unlikely pair together, the fortune
in sparkling jewelery could give
each woman what she desires most.
But the real treasure is the friendship
that forms when they discover that
all that glitters isn't gold.

Sparkle

by
Jennifer Greene

Home improvement has never seen results like this!

When she receives a large inheritance,
Stacy Sommers decides she is finally going
to update her kitchen. Her busy husband has
never wanted to invest in a renovation, but now
has no choice. When the walls come down,
things start to change in ways that neither
of them ever expected.

Finding Home

by Marie Ferrarella

Hearing that her husband
had owned a cottage in England
was a surprise. But the truly
shocking news was what
she would find there.

Determined to discover more about the cottage
her deceased husband left her, Marjorie Maitland
travels to England to visit the property—and
ends up uncovering secrets from the past that
might just be the key to her future.

The English Wife

by Doreen Roberts

HN47

Available June 2006
TheNextNovel.com

HARLEQUIN®
Next™

Is reality better than fantasy?

When her son leaves for college, Lauren
realizes it is time to start a new life for herself.
After a series of hilarious wrong turns,
she lands a job decorating department-store
windows. Is the "perfect" world she creates
in the windows possible to find in real life?
Ready or not, it's time to find out!

Window Dressing

by Nikki Rivers

Life.
It could happen to her!

Never Happened just about sums up
Alexis Jackson's life. Independent and
successful, Alexis has concentrated on
building her own business, leaving no
time for love. Now at forty, Alexis
discovers that she still has a few things
to learn about life—that the life unlived
is the one that "Never happened"
and it's her time to make a change....

Never Happened
by Debra Webb

Available July 2006
TheNextNovel.com

HN49

Sometimes you're up… sometimes you're down. Good friends always help each other deal with it.

Mood Swing

by Jane Graves

A story about three women who discover they have one thing in common—they've reached the breaking point.

Available July 2006
TheNextNovel.com

REQUEST YOUR
FREE BOOKS!

2 FREE NOVELS TO INTRODUCE YOU TO OUR BRAND-NEW LINE!

There's the life you planned. And there's what comes next.